MONSTROSITIES

Third Flatiron Anthologies
Volume 7, Book 22, Spring 2018

Edited by Juliana Rew
Cover Art by Keely Rew

Monstrosities
Third Flatiron Anthologies
Volume 7, Spring 2018

Published by Third Flatiron Publishing
Juliana Rew, Editor and Publisher

Discover other titles by Third Flatiron:

License Notes

Contents

*****~~~~~*****

5

Editor's Note

by Juliana Rew

Third Flatiron presents *Monstrosities,* a new anthology of science fiction, dark fantasy, horror, and humor, in which twenty international authors ventilate about their favorite "monstrosities"—things that are just too big or dreadfully obnoxious.

A big deal. In our lead story, a young lady named Malayaga wants to sell her motel. In "Chicken Monster Motel" by Keyan Bowes, the couple who purchase it get much more than they bargained for.

Big splashes. The greatly missed multi-Nebula Award winning Edward Bryant was the author of over a hundred short stories, and we are delighted to reprint "Winslow Crater," which truly packs a punch. In James Dorr's hilarious "Got Them Wash Day Blues, "an explosion of stinky laundry proves to be a big problem, unless you're lucky enough to have a cold.

Mass extinctions. If a soul weighs three-quarters of an ounce, counting everyone who ever lived, that's "Five Billion Pounds of Soul," according to Larry Hodges, whose red-suited Devil carries a rather heavy burden one snowy Christmas eve.

Too big for their britches. A shyster learns he has to deliver on his promises to the cult in Carl R. Jennings's "Sacrifice Needed, Alcohol Provided." A dying monarch gives the lie to the old "heavy lies the head" saying, in Liam Hogan's "This Tyrant Crown." A new hashtag finds its way into one of our stories, "#Notalltigers" by Mark Pantoja, which isn't entirely successful at dispelling a stereotype.

Monstrosities

Drop the big one? As the "ultimate weapon" ups its game over the eons, Ray Daley's "The Doomsday Machine Retires," deciding to draw the final curtain.

Cosmic drama. Beware that hit TV series you can't take your eyes off. "Alien TV Shows Are Bad for Your Eyes" says Brian Trent.

Shop til you drop. In Salinda Tyson's "The Great Mall," it's your duty to keep the economy growing, even if you never get to keep your swag.

All one big joke. A prank among killbot jockeys forms the mystery in Jennifer R. Povey's "Skywalker."

Oh the humanity. We are partial to stories that ask big ethical and anthropological questions. Ville Meriläinen ponders whether uplift of other species is a supreme goal. A swine foments a revolution in order to return to the good old days, in his parable, "Eaten." Sita C. Romero's tale from Mexican mythology, "Into Xibalba," considers a philosophical "trolley problem"—the sacrifice of one to save many. To become a goddess to all mothers, a woman must die in childbirth.

Breakthrough project. In Martin M. Clark's "The Emerald Mirage," Professor Prinz inspires another temporal quantum leap, but is reliving the past to revive an old love affair really a good use of mega-resources?

Of course, monstrosities can just be flat-out monsters. In Sharon Diane King's tasty "TidBits," a pair of carnivorous but feckless young Dreadfuls get lost in the woods and are tempted by a delicious house.

Big magic. We're inordinately fond of oddball "artifacts," such as found in series like "The Librarians," and "The Magicians," so we conclude with Julia August's adventure, "The Catacombs of Constitutional History," in which an ambitious grad student stops at nothing to find something new that will cement her career.

For our flash humor (Grins & Gurgles) section, we have Robert Bagnall's "New Shoes," whose grandkids marvel at how people used to shop. Barry Charman shows that a little "Kismet" is essential if you want to keep doing the same job for eternity. And finally, we close with two tiny tales, both involving cockroaches, yet utterly different from each other: "They Saw Me Coming" by Russell Hemmell, and "Bigger and Better Things" by Joseph Sidari.

We hope you'll enjoy these fanciful tales, artfully designed to expose humongous blunders and put them to rest. Sweet dreams.

Juliana Rew
March 2018

*****~~~~*****

Chicken Monster Motel

by Keyan Bowes

"It's my birthright!" says Jerry, unloading his mom's India Market groceries onto the counter. "Everyone knows about motels and Patels. Motel, Patel, they go together." He pronounces Patel the American way, Pat-ell, instead of the Gujarati way, Puh-tale.

His father frowns. "We want a different life for you, Jairam," he says firmly. "Your expensive education is for what?" The Patels had run three different motels, eventually cashing out before Jerry went to college. "You think motel goes with Patel? Doctor goes even better. Google Dr Patel. You will get 82 million hits, including your cousin Leela."

"Papa, I just graduated! I don't want to go to Med School. I didn't even write my MCAT!"

"Then you should write it!" His father storms out.

"I hate exams!" Jerry shouts after him.

...

Later, his mother hands him a jewelry box. "Jerroo, son, if that's what you really want, sell these, give it a try. I have faith in you."

"What, seriously?" Jerry opens the box to find twelve diamond-studded gold bangles. Two have elephant heads with emerald eyes. He's seen these on his mother's

11

wrist at his cousin's wedding. They were handed down to his mother by her mother and her mother before. "Ma, you can't!"

"Take it, son. In this country, when will I wear this kind of jewelry?" She looks at him seriously. "Running a motel is a lot of work, but a young man should work hard."

The Motel on Craigslist

"Hey Peter!" Jerry's looking at Craigslist. "Here's a motel! It's even got a cafe. Up in the mountains. We could do a road trip."

"What?" Peter says. "Dude, you haven't even got the jewelry appraised yet." He reads over Jerry's shoulder. "Weird name, Chicken Monster Motel."

"Gotta start looking, right? Let's go get a Starbuck's and plan the road trip." Jerry dumps his mug in the sink. "Ten minutes to pack."

"*Plan* a road trip, you said."

Jerry drops a kiss on Peter's neck. It leads to one thing and another and takes more than ten minutes.

But the packing doesn't. Toothbrush, smart phone, clean t-shirts, socks, and boxers. "Don't leave the jewelry behind in the empty apartment," Peter says. "And I'll drive. I don't want gray hair before I'm thirty."

Slow Season at the Chicken Monster Motel

"Finally! There it is." Jerry accelerates wildly around the curving mountain road. He's driving after all, and they're both frazzled. The motel is perched in an unlikely spot on a cliff above them.

Jerry brightens. "Bet it has terrific views."

"Hope it has cold beer," Peter says.

Jerry blows him a kiss. "Yeah."

12

Chicken Monster Motel

The Chicken Monster Motel is clearly having a slow season. Peter's Honda is the only car there. The manager—a young woman who snaps her gum and ends all her sentences with question marks—tells him to pull into the garage underneath the building. Then it's a hot shower, cold beer, and surprisingly good beef sandwiches on the house. Jairam's parents would be horrified that he's not vegetarian, so he hasn't mentioned it. Though he's devoted to them, there's a lot he hasn't said. No point upsetting them.

Jerry likes what he sees. Maybe he can get a really good price on the motel, since it's so remote? It's clean and in good condition, with neutral walls and industrial carpet. The manager says it has forty rooms, a lounge with a commercial kitchen, and a small owner's apartment.

Peter and Jerry settle into big fake-leather armchairs beside a window overlooking a gorge. River sounds drift up.

"Your idea wasn't so dumbass," Peter acknowledges.

Jerry takes a contented swig from the beer bottle. The sky behind the mountains is turning from pink to purple, when the building shakes.

"Earthquake!" he tells Peter. "Feel that?"

"Here? No way. Which fault?"

The manager pops her head in. "Can you, like, fasten your seatbelts? We're just warming up now and waiting for full dark."

"Hey, wait!" says Jerry, "What seatbelts? Why?"

"Like, on your seats? Maybe you're sitting on them?" The manager snaps her chewing gum. "I gotta see your car's secured, y'know?" The door clicks shut behind her.

"I've never heard of seatbelts for earthquakes," Jerry says.

"They told us, duck and cover. But she seemed pretty positive. And there *are* seatbelts." Peter fastens his.

13

The manager runs in again, rushes to the window, and closes it. "Uh-oh! Nearly forgot! Creates too much drag, you know?" She rushes out before they can ask her anything.

"Drag? In an earthquake? What?"

The building shakes again. The floor actually seems to tip. Jerry expects the chairs to slide, but they're bolted to the floor.

"Put on your seatbelt," Peter says. "Don't be an idiot. She knows something."

Jerry opens his mouth to retort, when Peter says, "Oh. My. God. What's that?"

"That" is a pair of huge wings that appear on either side of the motel, visible through the lounge's wall of windows. They look more like the wings of eagles than of airplanes, but the feathers seem metallic, like they might be made of aluminum alloys.

The motel gives an experimental flap or two, and then rises from the cliff-edge, into the nearly dark sky. Peter gasps.

"What the. . . !" Jerry exclaims. His dream motel climbs in a large spiral, bumping through turbulence from the wind currents blowing up the gorge. So much for a really good price. "What's going on? Where's the manager?" They stagger to the door. It's locked. The motel lurches.

"I'm going to throw up," says Jerry. "Do they have barf bags?" Peter hands him the waste-bin. They yell for the manager, but she doesn't show. Now what?

The motel flaps onward through the night. Eventually they fall asleep in their chairs.

Where's the Beef?

The motel makes a surprisingly gentle landing in a cow pasture, especially considering it lands on one of the cows. When Jerry and Peter recover, the door's open.

14

Outside, they find the manager butchering the animal in the early morning light.

"Good catch today," she tells them cheerily.

"Won't the farmer be mad about the cow?"

"Nah, it's included in the landing rights." She loads a large piece of cow onto a hand-truck.

"Yuck," says Peter, but he goes forward to help.

Jerry feels sick to his stomach. He eats beef just fine, despite his parents' beliefs, but dragging around bleeding bits of carcass is too much.

…

Over breakfast, the manager introduces herself. Her name is Malayaga Smith, and she inherited the motel from her mother.

"I'm sorry for your loss," Peter says politely.

"Oh, she's alive, she just pretended to die. She got bored and decided to travel. I think she's in Kazakhstan this week. I get random messages from her."

"Ah. Umm." Jerry has no idea what to say. He helps carry the dishes into the kitchen and takes a closer look at the stainless-steel appliances. High-end. Well-maintained.

"So, why do you want to sell?" Peter asks Malayaga.

"It's not my kind of life, this motel management. Don't get to meet people, you know? I mean, they're all just passing through. I'm young, I'm single. I want to pay off my student loans, go to New York, get a studio apartment and a proper job. I'll sell at any reasonable price."

"Awesome!" says Jerry, excited.

"We haven't even seen the financials," objects Peter. "You're jumping the gun, dumbass. Did you notice we're the only guests here?"

"I have all the details in Qakbooks," says Malayaga. "Last year's audited numbers. Also route maps and clearances and rights and stuff?" She gestures at a desk in a glassed-in cubicle. "It's all there. I'll pull it out."

"No point wasting time with the financials, stupid, unless we're interested in the deal."

"We?" asks Peter slowly.

"Yes," says Jerry impatiently. "We. Aren't you coming? Look, she wants us in the cubicle."

They pore over the details. The Chicken Monster Motel actually has a high occupancy rate. The customers paid in a variety of currencies, including old Roman silver, Mughal coinage, golden eggs, singing harps, and jeweled mechanical birds. Her spreadsheet meticulously converted them into U.S. dollars as of the transaction date.

Malayaga is happy to accept Jerry's bangles as payment. She's accustomed to accepting payments that aren't in dollars. There's some kind of valuation and validation routine.

"But, you gotta be sure, you know?" Malayaga says. "You can't change your mind after it's done. The Motel only moves forward."

"Jerry," says Peter, "Do you even know how to run a flying motel? At a profit?"

Jerry laughs. "We'll learn as we go along. I don't even know how to run a grounded motel. Do you?"

Peter shakes his head. "Me? Writing code, remember?" He pauses. "Do we have wifi?"

Malayaga nods. "Permanent wifi and cellular. It's kind of built in to the Motel. It always gets a good signal."

That clinches it. "Okay," says Peter. "I can write code in the sky. I'm down with this."

"This will be awesome!" says Jerry. "A flying motel!"

Jerry hands the bangles to Malayaga like the treasure they are. She puts them in a drawer that slides open, then automatically slams shut. Jerry looks concerned.

"Nah, it's okay," says Malayaga. "The Motel values, converts, and shunts it to my account. That should be paying off my student loans, like, right now."

They shake hands on the deal. "I'll show you how it operates," she says. "It's, you know, intuitive."

Language of the Heart

The control room door won't open. Malayaga makes crooning sounds in a mysterious language as she tries the knob. The glass door remains immovable.

"D'you have a key?" Peter asks.

"There's no keyhole, stupid," says Jerry. "Maybe it's jammed? Do you have some WD40?"

"What language were the words you said?" Peter asks Malayaga.

"Finnish," she replies. "But Russian works too."

"Wait, I need to learn Russian or Finnish so I can command this motel?" asks Jerry.

"He sucks at languages," says Peter.

"It's sorta, 'communicate'? Not command?"

"Yeah, okay. So do I?" asks Jerry.

"Can he just talk English?" asks Peter.

"Maybe?" says Malayaga. They all look at the recalcitrant door. The only sound is the snapping of chewing gum.

"What were you saying, anyways?"

"Open sesame," says Malayaga.

"Open sesame? In Finnish? That's from Arabian Nights, not anything Finnish or Russian."

"Yeah," says Malayaga, sounding baffled. "So?"

They take turns whispering, shouting, and singing Open Sesame. By the time Peter's doing it like phone sex, Jerry can no longer listen.

"Why'd you pick Finnish?" he asks Malayaga.

"It's gotta be, like, a language of the heart?"

Peter's seductive voice isn't getting anywhere with the door, but is having an effect on Jerry. He focuses on what Malayaga's saying. "A. . . language of the heart? Like Peter's doing right now?"

Malayaga shakes her head. "You know when a baby gives back love? Like they're one or two years old, and they have some words to say? The language they learn then? That's a language of the heart."

"Wait, what? Don't babies speak English?"

"This baby didn't," Malayaga says, pointing to herself.

"Oh. Mother tongue. You mean your mother tongue?"

"Maybe?"

"So why isn't it working for Peter?"

"Why isn't it working for me?" says Malayaga. "Maybe the motel isn't mine any more, but it's not yours yet." She looks worried. "That's kinda not good. Maybe dangerous."

Oh great. A ronin motel.

It's Peter who says, "So what language did you learn then? Gujarati or some other kind of Indian?"

"I don't know," says Jerry. "Gujarati? Hindi? And 'Indian' is not a language, stupid."

"I didn't say it was, dumbass. I know India's got a bunch of languages and Gujarati's just one."

"I was born in Mumbai, it could have been anything. Gujarati, Hindi, Marathi. Anyway, I forgot them all."

"So, call your mom."

Jairam calls home. But it's his father who picks up the phone, and he is furious.

"I can't stop your mother from giving you her jewelry, but she was always too soft with you! All these years I've worked for the sake of this family! I wanted to make you a doctor or at least a dentist. Now what? You are going backwards!"

"Papa. . . " says Jerry, trying to get a word in.

"What do you know about motels?" his father asks.

Jerry hopes he won't have to answer too many questions when he admits he's bought the motel. He's looked at the numbers. What else should he know about? Structural integrity? Foundation work? No, probably not that. Not termite inspections either. Anyway, it's all up in the air—well, not literally—until the Motel gives him access.

He doesn't want to admit that to his dad either. He can imagine him yelling, "You bought a mobile home as a motel? And you don't have the keys? You can't get in? What useless thing have you done with your mother's jewelry?"

Not that his father lets him say anything at all. "Do you know how much work it is to run a motel? How difficult it is to make a profit? Do you know how to buy a business or a building? You are just being foolish, and your mother is encouraging you." His father slams down the old-fashioned landline phone with an audible thunk.

Peter eyes him unsympathetically. "You should get your mom a cell phone, dumbass," he says.

"She has one. A smartphone with email and apps and everything. It's usually turned off. They like me to call the landline." Jairam tries his mom's cellphone, but she doesn't answer. He leaves a desperate message.

No Treasure, No Motel, No Chance

Jerry sinks back on the sofa in the motel lounge, staring out at the sunset and the unperturbed cows. The motel's still not responding. Malayaga's voice has gone from crooning to pleading, but the door remains shut.

The transaction is irreversible, the precious bangles gone to pay off Malayaga's student debt. All Jerry has to show for his mother's faith in him is an uncooperative flying motel.

Peter massages his shoulders. "I'm going to help Malayaga," he says. "Maybe we should kick the door down?"

Malayaga looks horrified. "You'd be so dead," she says. "I mean, like literally. Don't play games with the Motel."

"Dead?" asks Peter "What? How dangerous is this?"

"It's a monster," says Malayaga, sounding miserable. "If it goes feral and starts flying without a flight plan. . . "

Jerry's imagination completes the sentence in terrifying ways. What would happen if the Motel started flying barrel rolls? Or wandering off in random directions? Did it even need to stay in this world? Would it migrate or search for others of its kind? Would it care or even realize it had guests aboard?

"Maybe we should leave, you know?" Malayaga says. "While we can. I'll pack my bag. Your car got gas?" She disappears into the hallway, reappearing in minutes with a suitcase. "Come on!" she says.

"Wait," says Jerry. "Are we just going to abandon it? What happens next?"

"We'll figure that out," she says. "First, let's go!"

"Wait," says Peter suspiciously. "You got Jerry's treasure. Now you can't control the Motel. Maybe we all leave, and later you just call it to come get you?"

"It's seriously not a trick! Come on!"

But it's too late. The door locks. The motel lurches into the darkening sky. Malayaga falls into an armchair. "Fasten your seatbelts," she says quietly.

Peter turns pale, and Jerry swears under his breath.

Momma Ex Machina

Fortunately, except for some jolting due to air pockets or willfulness, the Motel flies quite steadily

20

through the night. By dawn, they make a rough touchdown in a deserted field, with no people or cows.

"Where are we?" asks Jerry.

Malayaga looks out the window and shrugs. "We'll find out when the doors open. And then we'll leave."

"Leave? Look, we're still alive. I'm not leaving!"

"Jerry," says Peter. "We don't know what it'll do tonight. We can't stay."

Jerry shakes his head stubbornly. "I'm not giving up on my dream!"

Peter looks somber. "Then I'll stay too."

…

Jerry calls home again, dreading another confrontation with his dad. The line is dead. Did Papa deliberately keep the phone off the hook? He'd been mad enough. Jerry's leaving another desperate message on his mother's cellphone when the phone rings in his hand.

"Jerroo. I found a message on my phone?"

"Mom? Thank you Ma, thank you thank you thank you!" He explains the problem.

"I see. You already bought a motel? Here is what you must say. Khulja simsim."

"Cool-ja sim-sim?"

Malayaga catches his eye and points at the control room door. It's swinging open. They all cheer.

"It opened? Good," says Mrs Patel. "Now go put some sandalwood paste on its forehead."

"Mom, I don't have any sandalwood and it doesn't have a forehead! It's a flying motel. Why are we putting sandalwood on it?"

"It's auspicious. Any good Indian store will have sandalwood." She pauses. "The jewelry box, I kept a little bit in there."

Malayaga brings it over. Sure enough, they find a tiny baggie under the red velvet lining.

"Good," his mother says. "I'm just now saying a small prayer to Sri Ganesh. We should invoke him before any project, I thought I taught you that much. He is Vigneshwara, the Remover of Obstacles."

Jerry smudges some of the fragrant paste on the control panel. He hopes it won't short-circuit anything.

...

"Hey, Peter? Thanks."

"What for, dumbass? I didn't do anything."

"You stuck with me. We were possibly going to die."

"Yeah, I'm not leaving you to die alone. Your parents would kill me."

Jerry drops to one knee, pulling a ring from his pocket. "This was going to be romantic, not just randomly in a flying motel. But Peter—will you stick with me forever? Will you marry me?"

Peter gulps and nods. "Yeah. Someone has to keep you out of trouble, or at least keep you company." He pulls Jerry to his feet and hugs him.

"Awww," says Malayaga. "You know, I think this motel's liking you guys already?"

Jerry blushes. "Our first home as a married couple!" he says.

"Congratulations!" Malayaga says, pulling out a bottle of champagne. "Drop me off in New York tonight? I've already packed."

###

About the Author

Keyan Bowes is a peripatetic writer of science fiction and fantasy based in San Francisco. She has lived in nine cities in seven countries, and visited many more. They sometimes form the settings for her stories. Her work can be found online in various webzines including a Polish one, a podcast, and an award-winning short film; and on paper in a dozen print anthologies. She's a graduate

Chicken Monster Motel

of the Clarion Workshop for science fiction and fantasy writers. Keyan's website is at www.keyanbowes.org.

*****〜〜〜*****

Winslow Crater

by Edward Bryant

METEOR

METEOR

METEOR

METEOr

METEOr

METEOr

METEor

METEor

METEor

METeor

METeor

METeor

MEteor

MEteor

MEteor

Meteor

Meteor

Meteor

meteor

meteorite

About the Author

The greatly missed Edward Bryant was the multi-Nebula Award winning author of over a hundred short stories, over a thousand essays and reviews, and one novel with Harlan Ellison, *Phoenix Without Ashes.* Ed's complete collected works are in the process of becoming available at the Reanimus Press website: http://ReAnimus.com/authors/edwardbryant. Reprinted with permission.

*****~~~~~*****

Five Billion Pounds of Soul

by Larry Hodges

Aza the Devil shook with fear in the intense heat of Hell. He hoped to blend into the fiery background with his red coat with white trim as he cowered in the hole he'd hurriedly dug with his powerful claws in the volcanic rock. White ash fell like snow from the surrounding fires. He has seen and especially heard the explosive arrival of the Big Gal of the Galaxy, and did what any intelligent life form does when the Big Gal comes looking for you—he hid.

"Come out, come out, wherever you are!" cried a high-pitched voice that obviously was not the Big Gal, whose voice was more like a foghorn on steroids. But Aza did not recognize the voice as one of his minions. Probably another mortal, using modern drilling equipment, had somehow found her way down to the underworld, perhaps in a pitiful attempt to bring back a loved one. Just what he needed, someone bringing attention to his hiding place. The Devil levitated up out of the hole, ready to smite the silly mortal before she gave his position away.

"Hi there, Hot Stuff," said the Big Gal herself, in the high-pitched voice. She was a willowy blonde in a black evening dress, swaying back and forth like a cobra locking onto its prey. Her cheekbones were so high they threatened to ambush her yellow eyes, stretching her cheeks so thin he could see the crooked, pointed teeth inside. "Hiding again?" She pointed a finger at him, freezing him in place before he could wriggle away. In her other hand she held, by their strings, a handful of colorful balloons.

"What happened to your voice?" he croaked, for he'd accidentally swallowed a fist-sized bit of ash. He grabbed at his throat with his thick claws. He vaguely resembled a man in the way that a shaved bear standing on its hind legs might. No red skin, no forked tail, no horns— those were human myths that came about from the Devil suit the Big Gal made him wear when interacting with humans. Just an invisible arm sticking out of his chest for grabbing souls. Aza's ancestors had evolved the arm to catch unsuspecting flying insects. It was why she'd picked his species, and unfortunately, him. Terrific.

She answered by dropping her lower jaw down like a snake and stuffing a balloon into it. There was a *pop*. "Helium balloons," she said, patting her skinny thighs. "Great low-cal snacks. Gotta watch the diet." She stuffed another into her mouth. There was another *pop*.

Aza took a deep breath of fresh burning brimstone. "What do you want?" It was disconcerting hearing that high-pitched voice coming out of that monster.

"Why do you assume I want something?" the Big Gal asked.

"Because you are here."

She nodded. "How true, and yet so quaintly insulting. So, how's the accounting?"

Perhaps all she wanted this time was a report. Last time she'd needed a volunteer to see if the inside of a quasar was hot. (It was.) The time before she'd wanted to test the effectiveness of various poisons she was considering for snakes and spiders. (They were.) And of course there was the first time, when she'd visited him in his nice mansion on a small planet circling Aldebaran to let him know she needed someone to watch over some new real estate she'd created. That's how he became the caretaker of Hell, deep in the center of the Earth, surrounded by artificial brimstone fires and way-too-bright electrical lights in the ceiling, where the only shower facilities were the surrounding magma. It seemed a lot of real estate for one beleaguered Devil and one large bottle.

"Since we started human collections 10,000 years ago I've collected 108 billion souls," he said. They were stored in the giant bottle carved from a black hole. The bottle was indestructible and soundproof, so he couldn't hear the lamentations of the departed in their prison. "Do you need exact numbers?"

"No, no," she said, nodding. "You've done well for a being that hasn't kicked a babby in years."

"Collecting over 150,000 souls a day isn't easy," he said, swelling with pride, while hoping she wasn't about to recruit him for one of her babby-kicking trips. It had been easier in the early days when there were fewer humans, and so fewer died each day. It had also been a long time since the Big Gal had complimented him. Why, the last time was when she praised how well he maintained his Aldebaran mansion. . . *Oh oh.*

"You're going to have to up your game," she said. "Remember that asteroid I threw that hit the earth 65 million years ago? Well, on that very same day, back in the Jurassic when you were ankle-high to a Tyrannosaur, I threw another rock. Seems like yesterday." The Big Gal had no time sense. To her, entire epochs flew by like dragonflies.

Then he stared at her. What was that about a rock?

"It was a big rock," she continued. "A really big one. I threw it from the center of the galaxy, 27,000 light years from here. It's been traveling through space at 77.3

miles per second ever since. And guess what? It's going to hit Earth in three years."

He stared at her. "How could you do that!"

"I have a very strong and accurate throwing arm."

"No, I mean *why* would you do that!"

"If you wanted to know *why,* why would you say *how*?"

He sputtered a bit.

"To answer your question," she said, tossing her blonde locks back with a toss of her head, "humans were born to die, and someone has to decide *when.* I made the decision, 65 million years ago, right after I killed the dinosaurs, that humans would be next. Or was it yesterday? No, it must have been 65 million years ago, or the rock wouldn't be so close already. And so humans evolved to die at the time I chose, three years from now."

"How big is this 'rock'?"

"Oh, 'bout the size of a golf ball."

He let out an involuntary but happy exhalation of brimstone smoke. Even at 77.3 miles per second a golfball-sized rock wouldn't cause much damage on a global scale.

"That's relative to the size of a basketball," she continued, "where Earth is the basketball. Should I yell *Fore!*?"

He did an involuntary inhalation and began coughing when he inhaled another large chunk of white ash.

"Yep, it's a lot bigger than that one from 65 million years ago. This one will utterly destroy Earth, killing all seven billion humans and everything on it. It'll be up to you to collect all their souls in one day, before they can float away into the comfortable vacuum of space. You know how souls are, always darting about like minnows, trying to get away."

"I can't collect seven billion souls in one day!" he exclaimed. *You monster!*

"What did you say?" she asked. She'd run out of helium and her voice was back to foghorn ferocity. She nonchalantly pointed a manicured finger at him and waved it about. His body waved about like a scarecrow in a hurricane. She pulled her finger down and he slammed into the ground, head first. She raised her finger and he shot into the air and into the cement ceiling of Hell.

"I said I'll collect all seven billion souls in one day," he said, rubbing his head and wishing he were back at Aldebaran. She lowered her finger and he fell to the ground, stubbing a toe in the process.

"Then I'll let you down, because I *know* you won't let me down." She disappeared in a fiery display that made the fires of Hell look like fireflies.

…

He would need lots of practice if he wanted to have any chance of collecting seven billion souls in one day. That meant multiple practice runs. But how could he do a trial run at collecting seven billion souls without first killing them?

He needed something that lived wherever there were humans, and large enough that its vestigial soul would be collectible. But what? Then he remembered that humans had pets. Lots of them! Perhaps puppies. He could cover the planet in a cloud of puppy poison to kill them all so he could collect their souls for practice. Or kittens. But puppies and kittens weren't popular enough— only a few families had them, which he found surprising since he found them so cute.

But there was an obvious option—babbies! Everyone loved these cute little mammals. They had the eyes of a doe, the body of a large hamster, and when happy—which was always—they both wagged their tails and purred. Nearly every household had a babby—seven billion in all.

So, early on the morning of December 24, Aza donned the itchy woolen red Devil suit that the Big Gal made him wear—hadn't she heard of polyester?—hopped onto a floating sleigh filled with babby poison, and took the secret tunnel to the surface. He flew all over the world, zigzagging about as he dropped the deadly poison everywhere. By that afternoon the world was filled with dying babbies and weeping children.

That night he did his first practice run. He was fighting a cold that made his nose red, and so he again put on his red coat with white trim. Flying and working faster than he had ever flown and worked before, he landed on top of every house in the world that had a babby, dropped down the chimney with a bag over his shoulder, and collected the babby souls with his invisible hand. It wasn't easy as the little things darted in every direction as he frantically chased them about houses, down streets, and up into the sky, grabbing at them with his invisible hand. Several times he painfully injured the hand grabbing at them in their babby exercise wheels.

It took him two days to collect them all—too slow. He needed more practice. He released the babby souls into space, and watched them scamper away at super-scamper speeds.

Meanwhile, humans mourned the loss of their babbies. Scientists figured out they'd been poisoned, and inevitably the finger-pointing began. The socialists did it. The capitalists did it. Libertarians. Drug cartels. Republicans. Democrats. Islamists. Jews. Homosexuals. The Americans. The Chinese. The North Koreans. Sasquatch. Little green men. A few even correctly blamed the Devil.

But humans were a resilient species. There were no more babbies, so they found a replacement—tutties. They were a prolific species of purple and yellow striped parrot from South America, with the same doe-eyed look of a babby. By some strange quirk of evolution or the work of the Big Gal, when they squawked it came out very clearly as "Love ya!" They wagged their tail feathers when humans approached, and yes, they purred. One year later, after a worldwide dedicated breeding program, there were seven billion tutties, and nearly every household had them.

Once again on the morning of December 24 Aza flew about the world, this time spreading tutty poison. This time it took him one and a half days and a painfully tired arm to collect all seven billion tutty souls. He needed more practice. He released the tutty souls into space, and watched them fly away at super-flying speeds.

The humans mourned the loss of their tutties, but once again they were resilient. They bred lallies as their next pet. A lally is a prolific species of a pure white snake from the Himalayas. They too had doe eyes—what is it with humans and the eyes of female deer? Like all snakes, they naturally wagged their tail side to side when they moved about. They loved to cuddle with humans, though some scientists speculated they were trying to crush the life out of the human but didn't have the strength of their constricting ancestors. Within a year seven billion of the cute serpents slithered about in nearly every household.

Once again on the morning of December 24 Aza flew about the world, this time spreading lally poison. He collected all seven billion lally souls in one day. His invisible arm felt like it was about to fall off, but he was ready.

After he gathered the last lally soul from an apartment in Chicago, the exhausted Devil sat on the floor, leaning against his sack, jammed full of lally souls. He could smell delicious odors from the kitchen—roast turkey and ham, eggnog, apple pie—and was thinking about raiding it before returning to Hell.

That's when he noticed the little girl in yellow Superwoman pajamas sobbing in the corner, hugging the body of a dead lally. The snake wore a wig of long, blue hair with a golden tiara with a red star on it—Wonder Woman dress up.

33

"Why are you crying, little girl?" Aza asked.

"Wondergirl is dead!" she wailed.

"But it's only a snake," he said.

She jumped to her feet and ran to him. At first he thought she was going to hug him, and he extended his arms. She whipped him across the face with the snake, probably leaving a mark.

"No, she's not!" she screamed. "She's a hero, and she's my friend!" He looked her over and could see the glow of her throbbing soul in her chest. He reached out with his invisible hand, but changed his mind and decided not to take it.

"I only killed him for practice so I could kill and collect human souls next year." Honesty was always the best policy. Or so he'd thought until she kicked him.

Hours later he still felt the throbbing pain down there where she'd kicked him. Best not get involved with the natives, he decided. After all, in one year they would all be dead and he'd be collecting their souls. Including this little girl's.

He returned to Hell to wait out the year. He released the lally souls into space, and watched them slither away at super-slither speed.

But a funny thing happened on the way to Hell. He couldn't get her tear-filled face out of his mind. He could see the snake wrapped around her neck and draped across her arms as she hugged the cold, dead reptile he'd killed.

Why was she so unhappy? Was it because her pet had been killed? No, it was because she remembered her pet, and knew it had been killed. It was the memory that made her unhappy.

Well, he may have to kill them all in one year, but he could at least make their last year more pleasant. After a few hours working on a new potion, once again he flew about in his sleigh, this time spreading a specially created forget powder. Soon humans had no memory of babbies, tutties, or lallies. But the humans simply would not give

34

up on having pets. This time they doubled up and bred billions of puppies and kittens. But he didn't need any more practice, so the puppies and kittens could live.

But only until the Big Gal's rock hit the Earth, killing all the puppies, kittens, and humans. And everything else. Even the cockroaches, which he thought might have been the humans' next pet, with their cute antenna and dark eyes—but alas, no doe eyes.

It just wasn't right. But what could he do about it? Soon the rock would arrive, on the next December 24. Even he didn't have the power to stop it. He lounged about in the heat of Hell, wondering what to do. He stared at the black hole bottle containing 108 billion human souls. A human soul weighs 21 grams, or three-quarters of an ounce. That's five billion pounds of souls. His eyes went wide—doe-eyed wide—as he did some quick calculations in his head. The math didn't lie.

He pulled the cork out of the bottle. As the souls shot out, he explained the situation. The final thing he did was point in the direction of the incoming asteroid, still a good ways off.

What happens when five billion pounds of souls smack into a giant asteroid, at high speed, at just the right angle?

It was a close call, but it just missed hitting the Earth. Sure, there were some violent tides as the asteroid shot by, and the floods killed off the goggies, a very cute species of doe-eyed frog that was beloved by children everywhere, and which were already beginning to replace puppies and kittens in their hearts. He flew over the planet spreading another specially made forget powder. The goggies were forgotten, and puppies and kittens once again held sway.

Then he returned to Hell to await the wrath of the Big Gal.

...

35

"*Aza!*" screamed the Big Gal. "*What have you done!*" She waved her finger in a circle as Aza spun about in circles, thirty feet in the air. "That's 65 million years of my time you've wasted!"

"Sorry." It was difficult apologizing while being spun in a circle high in the air.

"*Sorry?* That's all you've got to say for this minor inconvenience? I'd sentence you to oblivion inside the hottest quasar, but I need you to catch all the souls you let loose. And yes, it's impossible to be incinerated in a quasar, poisoned by every known and unknown poison simultaneously, slammed into neutronium at light speed, and twenty other impossibly torturous deaths at the same time, but I'm the Big Gal and I can do the impossible." She waved her finger down.

"I'll get started now," he said, covering his head with his hands as it slammed into the ground.

"You may think you've saved the humans, but not a chance," the Big Gal said. "I've got an even bigger rock in the center of the galaxy, and I'm going there now to throw it. In just 65 million years it's going to destroy Earth, and your precious humans will be dead. *Hah!*" She disappeared in a fiery display that made supernovas look like fireflies, on her way to the center of the galaxy, just minutes away for her.

The Big Gal never did have much of a time sense. If he could gather five billion pounds of soul in ten thousand years, how much could he gather in 65 million years? That's 6,500 times as long. In fact, with that much ballast, he wondered what would happen if it all collided with the Big Gal herself? He did a few calculations, and smiled.

###

About the Author

Larry Hodges is an active member of SFWA with 86 short story sales, including 23 "pro" sales—twelve to Galaxy's Edge and eleven others. His fourth novel, *When Parallel Lines Meet*, which he co-wrote with Mike Resnick and Lezli Robyn, came out in late 2017. His third novel, *Campaign 2100: Game of Scorpions,* came out in March 2016, from World Weaver Press. He's a graduate of the six-week 2006 Odyssey Writers Workshop, the 2007 Orson Scott Card Literary Boot Camp, and the two-week 2008 Taos Toolbox Writers Workshop. In the world of non-fiction, he's a full-time writer with 13 books and over 1,700 published articles in over 150 different publications. Visit him at larryhodges.org.

*****~~~~*****

Sacrifice Needed, Alcohol Provided
by Carl R. Jennings

Most of the blood missed falling into the ornate stone cup. The Grand Master hadn't anticipated that arterial spray would be so violent. He also was unaware of alcohol's effect as a blood thinner. But, to give him credit, he had never cut anyone's throat before, and the slice was clean.

Not that he told any of his followers this. As far as they knew (because he had constructed a careful backstory for himself and an ancient one for the organization he made up almost a year ago), he was an old hand at sacrificial murder. They watched with a combination of awe, horror, and, in one man's head, a guilty and worried arousal.

The Grand Master managed not to vomit when his hand was covered by the warm, sticky ichor. He was rather proud of that. He even made the desperate fumble to catch as much blood as he could in the stone cup look like a solemn and practiced action—something he thanked his previous life as a stage actor for.

Things had gone well up to this point: he had a nice compound in the country to live in, people to wait on his every need, and almost more sex than he could cope with. It was all about attention. Oh so much attention; something he had craved all his life. He had gone from a forgotten nobody on a playbill gracing the ground in a side alley to "Grand Master." It was delicious.

It had been easier to make a cult than he thought it would be. A certain type of person would follow any hack if they came with a credo and structure for their life. He bought a portentous-looking old book that nobody was allowed to look in, made up a cheap story about transcendence, and life was peaches and cream.

Or it had been, until recently.

What the Grand Master hadn't realized was that you could sell good smells all day long, but you had to produce something to eat eventually. His followers had started to become restless with an apparent lack of progress on the promised transformation to divinity, so it was time to throw them a bone.

The Grand Master put an ad on Craigslist. It was titled: "Sacrifice Needed, Alcohol Provided." In the body of the advert it read that someone was needed to be the "lynchpin in a holy journey into dimensions and pleasures untold." To appeal to an even wider audience, he had added that there would be booze aplenty to drink. He had figured that the title would be ignored by normal people and clicked on by either the homeless or the mentally ill— the kind that used library computers to look for something to feed the particular habits that made them socially unfit.

By the smell of the "sacrifice" lying on the second-hand kitchen table the Grand Master had set up in a clearing outside the compound, he had been homeless; the man's grey beard was long enough to soak up a lot of the blood that had been contained inside of him until recently, and his clothes looked like they had been rummaged from a donation box twenty years ago. Despite the transient man's appearing to have given up on a life that had given up on him quite some time ago, the man had a dynamic enthusiasm when it came to corner store whiskey—he had drunk almost all the bottles that the Grand Master had given him before he was rendered suitably unconscious.

Sacrifice Needed, Alcohol Provided

The Grand Master peered into the stone cup by the scant yellow-orange light given off by the Tiki Torches he had set up in a rough circle around the clearing. There wasn't much blood in it, but his hand and the outside was coated in the stuff. It'd do to give a convincing performance. When nothing happened, as he knew it wouldn't, he'd blame his congregation for the ritual's failure—saying that one or all of them didn't believe enough. It'd cause enough suspicion and fear, that he would stoke within the appropriately dedicated people, to buy him another year of the easy life. After which he would have to think of something else to do to placate everybody, but that was down the road.

The Grand Master became aware that the nameless transient's dead eyes were staring directly into his groin. It was, to say the least, unsettling, and seriously threatened to diminish any unclothed rendezvous later that night. Seeing that the blood was now just a steady stream soaking into the grain of the table, the Grand Master turned the homeless man's head away from him as discreetly as he could.

He took a deep, steadying breath and spun around theatrically to face his congregation. He held the blood soaked cup high above his head. It was a good image: the be-robed Grand Master holding up the bloody cup in the light of the torches. The crowd gasped appreciatively— this is what they had gotten into this whole thing for. Up until now, it had been more like a summer camp, where the campers played combination palace servants and harem. A few had started getting suspicious that it was all a scam, but their ringing alarm bells were silenced now.

Employing the tone he used for Mark Antony in that disastrous abortion of a *Julius Caesar* production in Philly, the Grand Master intoned, "The Sacrifice has been Given!"

You could even hear the capitalizations. This aligned with the collective idea the crowd had about how

41

a sacrificial ceremony should go. Not that any of them had any firsthand experience, but they had all seen movies, and how different could it be, really?

The Grand Master ran through the hastily made-up ceremony in his head. It went as follows:

Okay, so I've cut the throat. Nothing to worry about there—that homeless guy's better off dead. He'll probably smell better as a corpse anyway. Then I held the cup up and said the thing, waited for the gasp, there could have been some applause but what are you going to do, now what? Oh yeah.

Out loud, he said, "We, the most Ancient Order of Benighted Seers call forth. . . " Pause for effect. He was quite proud of "Benighted." None of them had caught it, and it gave him a nice, private chuckle at the gullibility of humanity. He finished his sentence, his voice seeming to sweep at the crowd right through the dark woods, ". . . The Other Ones!"

The Grand Master upended the cup with a flourish, spilling the rapidly congealing blood on the ground. He felt that it made a rather lame pattering sound, but that might work in his favor. What he had planned next was to wait expectantly along with the crowd. When nothing happened, he would furiously accuse them of not believing enough and ruining all of his "efforts." He would then storm off in a swish of robes, and the congregation would decide on a spokesperson to come talk to him. He hoped it would be Madeline; that scarlet-haired honey who set off any number of fiery passions in him.

Unfortunately for the Grand Master, something did happen.

A burst of absolutely pure white light hit the clearing, near the far end of the crowd. It brought with it a noise that could be accurately reproduced by scraping a violin string with a knife while, at the same time, popping bubble wrap. Later, most of the congregation agreed that it was an A-string, but one of them insisted it was a G. By pure coincidence, that person was Madeline. If the Grand Master had been in any state at that time to hear her say the word "G-string," he would have suddenly needed a change of underwear.

The light faded, and the strange sound cut off abruptly. Now added to the congregation was the most curious creature that anyone present had ever seen and deserves recounting in detail: it stood on two thick, powerful-looking legs; two long spindly arms were held out in front of it bent at the wrists. It looked a green scale's thickness over six feet tall, exactly the kind of green scale that covered its body. Its long muzzle was wrapped in what looked like a shining metal cup with a speaker grill at the bottom; the cup extended up to cover its narrow, wedge-like face. Two yellow slits looked out of two glass lenses in the mask on either side of its face, and a tall, thin fin sprouted out of the top of its head.

The creature's groin area was covered in a shiny purple, bathing suit-like garment. Little attention was given toward clothes beyond the practical, such as the air-scrubbing device covering this creature's muzzle and the transparent protective polymer coating on its scales. The purple pseudo-Speedo was there for the convenience of the other species the reptilian creatures worked with who were not so socially forward thinking, and were apt to be distracted by green scaly genitals to the point that it was detrimental to any work that needed to be completed.

None of the crowd, including the Grand Master, could speak through their wide-open mouths. Fortunately for the continuation of the narrative, the creature did say something. Its voice was a little tinny as it came through the speaker of the mask.

"My goodness!" it said, sounding pleasantly surprised, turning its head from side to side so each eye could look at the people looking at it, "I didn't expect anyone to be here."

The clearing was silent, until the Grand Master let out a piercing scream.

"It actually *worked*?" he shouted when he was able to draw a breath again. "This wasn't supposed to be *real*! I just made it all up!" He tried to flee, but ran into the table. He knocked it over and fell on top of the homeless man's body.

The creature's bifurcated attention was directed in the Grand Master's direction.

"Well gosh, I'm sure I don't know what you mean by that," it said, as friendly as a call center support rep on their first day, "but I hope that everything you're doing goes swimmingly. I'll be out of your dewlaps in a moment, I just need to take a reading."

From a belt that was wrapped around its body just above its muscular haunches, it unclipped a small rectangular box with what looked like a microphone on top. It sculled around the clearing with a flashing speed, sending the congregation backpedaling away from it. While it moved around, the creature made one-way small talk with the crowd, while not taking its focus away from the device in its clawed front paws.

"My word, it's cold. No wonder you're wearing those long robe things. I couldn't stand it either!"

"Did you all pilot those combustible things here? What do you call them? Cars! That's it! I swear I'd forget my fin if it wasn't attached, ha, ha."

"I really don't mean to be a bother, but could you move aside for a second? Whoops, what a tumble! Are you alright?"

"You can never really get the destination just right on these Mark Forty-Two Portal Generators. They say they're more accurate than the old Model Seventy-Sevens, but I don't know."

When it seemed to be satisfied, it clipped the small device back on its belt.

"Alright, I'm off," it said, brightly, "Sorry again for bothering you."

It turned around and started to fiddle with something on the front of its belt. Its hitherto unnoticed tail swished gently back and forth. The congregation looked at the Grand Master for guidance. He was peering over the table, wide-eyed at the creature, unable to move. Silently coming to an agreement among themselves by means of eye contact and facial expressions, a spokesman stepped forward from the crowd.

"Um," he quivered at the creature, "Excuse me."

The creature's head tipped backwards so that one of its eyes was looking at the spokesman upside down. "Yes?" it said.

The spokesman nearly fainted, but rallied, swallowed audibly, then continued, "Aren't you going to take us with you? We're the ones who summoned you and all."

The creature's head righted itself as he spun around to face the spokesman. "I'm sorry?" It said, confused, "I'm not sure what you mean. Summoned me? This was a scheduled atmospheric check."

"But," the spokesman stammered, "the Grand Master said that this was a ceremony to summon beings from beyond the veil of space and time that would take us to a place of wonderment and joy beyond the limits of our imagination."

"Oh!" the creature said, "That sounds delightful!" It looked around with darting head movements as if it would find a paradise hiding behind a Tiki Torch. "It doesn't appear to have worked; everything looks normal to me."

"We thought you were going to take us there."

"Me?" It touched what would be a chest on a human with a clawed paw. "Oh, no, I'm afraid not. Like I said, I'm just here to check the progress."

"What progress?" the spokesman said, bewildered as the rest of the crowd.

"Why the terraforming, of course," the creature said. When it noticed that there was still confusion, it went on. "I work for a company that plops down a humanoid species on a planet and waits for it to reach its industrial age. It then pumps enough carbon dioxide into the atmosphere to change the air composition and temperature to something more suitable for us to live in. Once the population dies off, we come in and colonize the planet. Tremendously cost effective if you've got the patience for it."

Each face in the crowd looked at the creature with a variety of horrified expressions. Misinterpreting their distress, the creature soothed, "Don't worry, things are going along just fine! It shouldn't be much longer now!"

Before anyone could ask any clarifying questions, a section of the creature's belt beeped.

"Ah, it's ready!" it said. "You guys could get back to your 'summoning' thing now. Gosh, aren't you just the cutest!"

With that the creature turned. There was another flare of bright light and the sound that was most definitely an A-string, no matter what Madeline thought. When it all ended, the creature was gone.

The human mind is a wondrous thing, able to perform a staggering number of fantastic feats. But, at no fault of its own, one thing it can't do is quickly process an event that is wildly outside its field of experience. In these instances, it searches around for something that it can easily understand, so that it can later work up to the bigger conundrum.

In this instance, the hooded heads of the congregation eventually turned to look at the Grand Master. He was still shielded behind the table and crouching on top of a rapidly cooling corpse. The elected spokesman from before put voice to what they were all thinking.

"Tell us again," he said, his voice dripping with barely contained, outraged vitriol, "about this ancient and secret ceremony thing."

About the Author

Carl R. Jennings is a man who sometimes arranges words in interesting ways, but, more often than not, they're merely confusing and unsettling. Carl has been published in numerous magazines such as *Bête Noir* and *Grievous Angel,* and in several anthologies from companies such as Shadow Work Publishing and Gehenna and Hinnom. For even more useless information, please "like" Carl's Facebook page, or follow him on Twitter @carlrjennings.

*****~~~~~*****

#NotAllTigers

by Mark Pantoja

I first saw him at one of Brad and Allison's wine-and-cheese get-togethers. He was hard to miss, what with him being a three hundred and fifty pound tiger dressed in a sharkskin suit, tie loose around his neck, like he'd just gotten done with a long day of software sales. Seemed a bit formal for the party, or I was underdressed, which usually happens, since I pretty much only wear track suits. And by pretty much I mean exclusively.

The wine was whatev, but Allison had this goat gouda I couldn't get enough of. I was that guy hanging out by the cheese table all night.

The tiger towered over everyone else, tripodded up on his hind legs and tail, except for Rahul who was the same height, minus the tiger's ears on top.

The tiger pulled out a really long cigar and lit it up in the middle of the party. It stank up the room and set a hazy cloud over the party. People gave him ugly glances, and Allison got theatrical with a coughing fit, but the tiger didn't notice. And no one was actually going to say anything to him. He was a fucking tiger. He preferred cigars cause his fat digits couldn't hold a cigarette very long without getting singed, though I did see him smoke a roach that night, tweezed delicately between two razor sharp claws.

The tiger wobbled unsteadily when he walked upright and so usually took to all fours, though that night he was on threes, holding his cigar and a glass of red in his left paw. Even so, he slinked through the crowd with ease, blending his movement to the herd.

"Nice suit," he said as he slid up against the wall next to me. We made small talk. He spoke British English. It wasn't his mother tongue. Roaring was. His chuckle rattled the walls. It was basically just a shorter, more jovial roar.

He told me about growing up in Vietnam, in Phong Nah-Ke Bang National Park. He took English lessons to get a job in the states with Ringling Bros. He prided himself on his enunciation and bristled when anyone made lolcats jokes. (Seen him stare down a neck-beard with a "I can haz cheezburger?" t-shirt, who got so sweaty and nervous under the tiger's eyes he locked himself in the bathroom and didn't come out until we left, much to the annoyance of those outside banging on the door, doing the pee-pee dance.)

He was the coolest guy in the room. Moved like slow water and caught everyone's eye. Except when he didn't want them to. He could hide his bulky 500-pound frame in juniper bushes on the side of the road or behind the couch at a crowded get-together. It was uncanny, and a neat party trick.

He was charismatic. When you spoke he gave his total attention, as if your words dripped with gold. I'd say he had animal magnetism, but I think that's racist. And that night he was talking to me, listening to me, the guy by the cheese table, bogarting the goat gouda and nursing my wine so long a red ring had formed on the inside of the glass and my fingers had greased up the sides with cheese oil. I was just starting to wonder, when he laid it on me.

#Notalltigers

"I got this idea for an app," he said. Actually he had three. One was a fitness app. The other was a fitness and dating app. And the last one was a recipe swap app. Which could easily be tweaked into a dating app. Or a fitness app. It was a pitch, really. And I suspected it was the real reason he was talking to me. Someone (Brad) must have told him I'd made an app. I hadn't actually. I spent five years on a team and then quit, but still everyone thought of me as That App Guy. That was two years ago. I've been living off stocks since. You might have heard of the app. It's called Bummr. Yeah, that one. Lately I've been taking woodworking classes. And sleeping a lot.

"Oh," I said when he was done with his spiel.

"That's it? Oh?"

"No, it's just—" My face went flush. My daddy had one piece of advice when I was a kid: don't piss off a tiger. "I thought—well, I just thought you'd do something more. . . tiger-ish."

His pupils opened, turning into dark pits, his ears went flat against his head.

"Tiger-ish?" he said. "Tiger. . . ish?"

"Well, no, I just meant—uh—"

"Is that all you see when you look at me?"

"Well, no, I—" I took a deep breath, "A recipe-swap dating app? That's. . . that's not bad."

A smile cut across his face, revealing large canines and other sharp teeth, which left me cold.

He laughed and shook the walls and slapped a paw against my back.

We were friends.

. . .

"Hit it," he said later that night in the bathroom. Some girl was pounding on the door but the tiger had a line of coke laid out on Allison's marble sink. He held out a silver straw. For me. "Oh. The drip." He pinched his nose and snorted. But there was still some whiteness on his whiskers.

51

Everyone wanted to be his friend. Everyone wanted to be close to him (and at the same time wanted to run from him), but it was me he was hanging out with. It was like the coolest guy in school wanted to be my friend. I was so close I could smell that animal scent, almost horse-like, like wet grass, coming off him. I wondered, Grass? Perhaps he'd just eaten horse.

I was that close to him. To someone that cool. Someone that deadly.

...

He crashed that night at my place. Said he had some trouble with his roommates. ("Me, they said that I was the aggressive one. I wasn't the one who left passive-aggressive notes around the house about shedding too much. Never once did I mention how they always clogged the shower with their hair. Gross.") He stayed on the couch, and the night turned into a few days, which turned into a week, which turned into a month. And then my roommate Adam up and decided to move out. Didn't like a tiger hanging out in our house all the time.

"Obviously, he's racist," the tiger said when I told him about Adam.

In truth, the tiger wasn't a great roommate. Bit of a mess and laid around all day in the sun. When he sat on the couch he took up the whole thing. He had some kind of settlement from the circus. Something about his back. He nursed it with oxy and alcohol. Most mornings he was hung over and growling.

The morning of our investor meeting—for our recipe-swap dating fitness app—I founding him puking in the kitchen sink.

"In the sink?" I said.

He retched again and wiped his mouth with the back of his paw.

"Sorry," he said. "I can't fit in the downstairs bathroom."

It's true. He couldn't.

#Notalltigers

He splashed water on his face. It glistened on his whiskers. He kept looking out the little window above the sink.

"Want I should fix you some eggs?" I said.

He was a pescatarian. When he told me that I responded with surprise. I thought tigers had to eat meat, carnivores and such.

"Not all tigers," he said. "And fish are meat, too, buddy."

"You don't like meat?"

"It's not that. When people see me, all they see is an animal, dressed up in a suit, yeah, but an animal. But when I see other animals, all I see is myself. Except fish. They have dead eyes. So, you know, I don't feel bad eating them."

"What about me?" I asked him.

He shrugged. "Sometimes you have dead eyes, but I'm no man-eater."

"No," I said. "What do you see when you see a human?"

"I see hairless apes. Stuck-up hairless apes."

I had to get him freshened up for the big meeting so I put on a pot of water and ground some coffee beans.

It was easy to get people interested in his app. Well, not his app per se. His app sounded terrible. Which means, sounded like a typical app. ("Bummr: How bad was your day?") But no, he had something different. He had that thing, that thing that investors look for, that buyers want, that marketers dream of. He had pizazz. Because he was a fucking tiger. A real tiger. Tony the Tiger launched a whole brand. A real tiger could run a corporation. Or at least, that was the hope.

"You're a good friend, you know that?" he said when he came into the kitchen and smelt the coffee in the air.

"Thanks," I said.

"I'm going for a walk," he said. He moved lazy and heavy, but without sound. I watched him from the kitchen window disappear into the shrubs out back. He wasn't coming back, I thought, and it felt true.

I went into his room later, ostensibly to clean it up since he wasn't coming back. There were a lot of beer bottles and little plastic Jim Beam flasks. And discarded animal bones. Gnawed-on cow bones wrapped in dirty sheets and stuffed under his bed, the bed that he'd ripped apart to make a nest. The room reeked carnivore.

I thought about setting the house on fire, but that was arson. And a bit dramatic. And final. What if I changed my mind?

The tiger left me alone in my house.

So I followed him out into the wild.

...

I spent three years there. Living in the forest, eating insects and grubs and tubers and befriending wolves and fighting bears. I followed my friend the tiger's life. I was inspired. I lived. That's more than most can say.

But I was called out of the wild. Student loans. Those fuckers don't ever give up.

When I came out of the openness of pure freedom and into the closedness of the city, my first stop was a Starbucks. For three years I'd had an itch I couldn't scratch: pumpkin spiced Frappuccino. You can't get that in the forest.

And while waiting in line I saw a newspaper out on a table. The tiger was on the cover of the business section. StripeSwap.com just got bought up. For a billion and change. The tiger had never gone back to the wild. He had just moved. Left me behind.

I thought about this for a while. Sipped my Frappuccino and pondered.

In the end, I didn't figure much out.

###

About the Author

Mark Pantoja is a graduate of the Clarion West 2011 Workshop. He has published stories in *Lightspeed Magazine*, *GigaNotoSaurus,* and NewMyths.com.

*****~~~~*****

The Doomsday Machine Retires

by Ray Daley

Twenty thousand years really isn't much, not in terms of a civilization, at least. Nations may rise and fall. In fact, they almost certainly will and have done. Factions grow, only to vanish like they had never existed in the first place.

Twenty thousand years is also just long enough for an idle doodle on the back of a coffee stained disposable napkin to become a fully fledged, warts-and-all Doomsday Machine.

But I'm still not exactly sure why they decided to call me Nigel?

Constructing any device capable of ceasing totality in an instant is quite the long-term commitment, both in terms of time and money. When you want all the bang there is and ever will be for your buck, you need to spend quite a few bucks indeed. Also, it's not just a case of your species saying,"We simply can't live with you in the same Universe any more."

It's more like your species saying, "If we can't wipe out all other intelligent lifeforms around here, then no bugger gets to call this Universe home, not even us!"

It's far beyond cutting off your nose to spite your face. It's more akin to cutting off your entire head, slicing it up into little bits and then feeding those bits into a mincer to spite your face.

Frankly, it's more than just a little bit bloody silly.

...

But build me they did. Nigel, the Doomsday Machine. *I think, therefore I doom.*

But not so far.

Across the vastness (relative to an organic life form) of 20,000 years, there's always some joker who wants to make a minor addition or alteration to your design. So, every thousand years or so I'd get a ship brimming full of that particular generation's finest military minds arriving to ask me if I had a Zeta Wave Particle Displacer or whatever weapons technology might be currently *en vogue.*

And me being the honest young Doomsday Machine that I was on their very first visit, I said, "No sir, I haven't got one of those."

So, with disgust at my seemingly primitive destructive technology, my activation date was duly postponed until the finest military minds of the age were all absolutely one hundred percent satisfied that I was the best and most powerful totality destroying device that had ever existed. And with that one simple question began an almost unending cycle that continued across the next nineteen thousand years.

...

Old military minds die, and new ones are born. Ones that grow up thinking thoughts like "our Doomsday Machine really needs a Hyper-phased Obliteron" or some other such nonsense like that.

A thousand years flashed by for a sentient killing machine capable of bringing about the end of everything that exists. Including chicken soup. Excuse me for mentioning it but my creator, now long since dead and turned to dust rather liked drinking chicken soup.

I was beginning to miss him, and our little chats across a cup of piping hot chicken soup.

...

As each new generation made my abilities increasingly more deadly, I began to develop a rather negative (and some might say unhealthy) attitude to my original purpose and entire reason for being. In fact, on one of those upgrade visits I made a point of asking one of the latest military minds exactly what was the point of building a weapon that would destroy everything, not just their enemies?

Without a moments hesitation he said, "Well our enemies will all be dead!"

I pointed out, "As will you, and your entire civilization sir. Isn't it just a touch of overkill?"

The military mind in question duly told me there was no such thing and that I shouldn't spend any further time worrying about it. It simply wasn't part of my job.

But worry I did. You see, the trouble with making your Doomsday Machine sentient is we do the exact same silly things that organic sentients do.

Like worry, and have self doubt. And existential crises. But I'd also been told by the owner of that military mind to shut up and just do my damn job when push finally came to shove.

...

After fourteen thousand years of constant upgrades I was finally asked a rather interesting question.

"Do you have every available weapon in your arsenal with which to destroy our enemies?" They then added, "because frankly, we'd quite like to be rid of them now. Like today, in fact. Now. If not sooner."

You see, another issue with having a sentient Doomsday Machine who's already had fourteen thousand years to mull over an existential crisis is it realises when its constructors say they really want to destroy everything, you rather quickly begin to understand that a very large portion of the everything they'd like to destroy also happens to include that very Doomsday Machine itself.

And I'd rather come to enjoy existing. Even if I didn't have any chicken soup to talk across. Piping hot or otherwise.

So, when they asked me about having all the weapons, I truthfully said "no." Of course I didn't currently have *every* weapon at my disposal.

After their furious outbursts (which also including shooting at me) I packed them all off to the historical archive to fill the apparent "gaps" in my weapons array. Many of the items listed were sheer fool's errands, being utterly useless in the endgame of destroying all existence.

For example, the humble cannonball has no place in the annihilation of everything, but I made them rediscover the techniques for its creation and implementation (the practical upshot of which brought about the discovery of a cure for a previously incurable disease). Their history showed them who they had once been, a formerly proud nation of intelligent peaceful beings.

And a rather small number of them suddenly didn't like seeing what they had now become in their fervent quest for total destruction. That small number were extremely vocal about their displeasure. But they gradually became louder and a good deal more influential in political circles which were the ones that actually mattered.

I tried my best to delay my activation even further by suggesting additional weapons, until it finally came to the point where there was only one offensive item left that I didn't possess.

The military minds were quite frustrated by this juncture and quizzed me on the matter. "And what might that be, Nigel? A fairly heavy rock? Harsh words?"

The Doomsday Machine Retires

I helpfully pointed out that I already had thirty-eight million rocks of various weights and sizes as well as a large number of extremely harsh words from numerous cultures all now long lost to posterity. Sadly, the military minds didn't comprehend irony or sarcasm and were insistent to know precisely what this final item was.

"A sharp stick sir," I told them. Then followed much explanation as to what one was and its source. They all rushed off to find the nearest tree to chop down, sharpen, and finally have me doing the job I'd been built for. So the finest military minds had to travel for 3,000 years to find a planet that still *had* trees.

…

And find it they did, duly assisted from co-ordinates supplied by me. Their ship finally reached orbit around a planet that is now rather kindly named after me. There's an *extremely* good reason behind that.

I'd had 17,000 years to reach the point of complete understanding by then. I had finally worked out that the folks in our adjacent system weren't the actual source of our conflicts.

It was the bloody military minds causing all the damn trouble!

And by sending them off to only I knew where, I had all of them in one place at the same time, completely at my mercy.

The thing about military minds, they really didn't get the concept of mercy, what with the whole spending 17,000 years creating the ultimate Doomsday Machine and all.

I wished to continue to exist. So, in order to achieve this I had to destroy the greatest threat to my creators.

Who were in turn, my creators. No, not the chap who liked chicken soup, but the screaming horde of uniformed low-browed fools who stole his idea and set about making it a reality. The military minds.

So, as they reached an intercepting orbit around a pleasant arboreal planet now called Nigel, they suddenly found themselves being targeted by every weapon known to civilization bar the sharp stick.

Their strongest and best shields held out for all of an entire pico second.

Then they found themselves being bombarded by almost everything including thirty-eight million rocks of various weights and sizes, as well as a kitchen sink. Their instrument of destruction proved to be the end of them. I rather liked the irony.

...

Over the next three thousand years, I spent almost every hour explaining my actions to the very people they had given their very lives to defend.

Questions were asked of me. Questions like "But every weapon you had? Wasn't that just a touch of overkill?"

At that exact moment I was so glad that I'd recorded every conversation I'd ever had up to that point. I still replay that conversation now, when people mention the term.

So, now we have a golden age of peace. I keep an eye on any aggression, but on the whole, nobody dares to lift a finger against anyone else now. Mostly down to my actions three thousand years ago.

It's awfully quiet now.

And there are certain days where I'd given anything for a sharp stick.

Just the one, mind! *I can't abide overkill.*

###

About the Author

UK writer Ray Daley was born in Coventry and still lives there. He served six years in the RAF as a clerk and spent most of his time in a Hobbit hole in High Wycombe. He is a published poet and has been writing stories since he was ten. His current dream is to eventually finish the Hitch Hikers fanfic novel he's been writing since 1986. Visit his website at https://raymondwriteswrongs.wordpress.com/. His Twitter handle is @RayDaleyWriter.

*****~~~~~*****

Alien TV Shows Are Bad For Your Eyes

by Brian Trent

Former SETI employee Dr. Brent Stone had been watching the alien signals longer than anyone else in the world—five weeks, that's a full two weeks before they were disseminated to the public—so maybe *that's* why he had a third eye growing out of his forehead.

Oh, he was trying to conceal it with his hair, going for the brushed-forward, hipster-out-of-bed look to hide the monstrous alien organ puckering in the center of that deeply lined, fleshy expanse. But the guy was balding. His thinning, sandy-blond locks were like a threadbare curtain over the horrible, inhuman, third eye.

I smiled politely in his doorway. "Dr. Brent Stone?"

The astronomer gave a boyish grin. "That's me! Come in!"

The interior of his California ranch resembled the aftermath of several overstuffed closets projectile vomiting all at once. I couldn't believe that tidying the place up, *knowing* that he was going to have a visitor today, hadn't crossed his mind.

"So, what are your favorite programs?" Stone asked.

"Well," I said, regarding his triple-stare, "I think it's a tie between *Glak* and *Veerdo's Spatlings*. And I

65

know everyone's wild about *Turb*—you know, that show with the mountain-size slug-things constructing some kind of mucous-ladder to the moons—but I missed the first few episodes, and I want to see them in order. I hate watching TV shows out of order. It ruins the entire experience."

"That's true!" the astronomer said with a winning smile. "But you really should check out *Turb* anyway. It has the best writing of any extraterrestrial channel we know of. Snappy dialogue, man! You should *make* the time to catch up!"

"I should," I admitted, having heard really good things about that particular signal piping down to us from Gliese 667.

Dr. Stone plopped onto an unsightly yellow couch and cracked open a can of cheap beer. "Can I get you anything to drink? Or did you want to dive right into this interview? I gotta say, fame is strange! Going from being night-shift manager at SETI to the discoverer of extraterrestrial radio signals is not exactly how I imagined this year developing!"

"I'm sure," I said and cracked open my notebook. "So, about that third eye growing out of your forehead. . . "

The astronomer gave a surprised, embarrassed start. "Is it *that* obvious? I thought I had been hiding it."

"Well I can see where you were *trying* to hide it. But to be honest, and please don't take offense at this, you're totally going bald."

He shook his head in disappointment. "You know, twenty years ago I would have been able to hide that third eye without a problem. I had hair like a lion's mane! I could have been a glam rocker!"

"You could always try Propecia or Rogaine," I suggested.

He clucked his tongue. "Nah, I'd rather grow old gracefully. No point in messing with the natural order of things, right?"

"Why *do* you have a third eye?" I asked, steering the conversation away from pedestrian small-talk.

"Don't know," he shrugged. "It started about a week ago."

I took up position on the couch across from him, considering this. "A week ago," I repeated, doing the math. "Meaning that one week from now, the rest of the world will have caught up to the amount of exposure that you've had?"

"Yep, that sounds about right." He put his feet up on the table and folded his hands across his belly.

"Um. Does it sound reasonable that long-term exposure to these signals is responsible for your. . . mutation?"

Brent Stone scratched his tangle of thinning hair. "Probably. I mean, third eyes don't exactly run in my family."

I twirled my pen in my hand, realizing I hadn't written anything in my reporter's notebook yet. "These alien shows are fairly popular now," I managed.

"You can see why! They're *awesome!*"

"That's not what I'm getting at."

He raised an eyebrow in surprise. The expression caused his third eye to squint as if trying to focus on something very far away. "Oh?"

"If it takes five weeks of exposure to grow a third eye," I said, trying to be as diplomatic as possible, "Then what happens next week when the global populace has been exposed to the same amount that caused *you* to change?"

He stopped scratching his head. "Ah! I see where you're going with this." He took a hearty, messy sip of his beer and switched on the TV. Weird, scintillating colors swirled across the screen.

I let the silence gather around us, like the motes of dust drifting through the stuffy air. Beams of sunlight stabbed in through the windows to create bright puddles on the boxes and other clutter.

I cleared my throat. "Do you think. . . I don't know. . . maybe we should *tell* someone?"

He looked confused, and the third eye in his forehead wrinkled. "Well I *guess*."

"Doesn't having a third eye bother you?"

"You know, I always thought that a forehead needed *something*. Foreheads are like blank walls in want of a painting. And I should know!" He pointed to the desolate, peeling walls of his shoddy living room. "Also, to be honest, I've always *wanted* blue eyes."

"You don't have blue eyes, Dr. Stone. You have a single blue eye that lacks an iris or pupil, sitting there like a huge blister in the center of your forehead."

The astronomer gave a disappointed sigh and sagged his shoulders. "See, I thought it balanced the other eyes nicely."

"Well, it *would*," I admitted. "Except that it's clearly an *alien* eye, so it doesn't really match. Like, at all."

The silence returned, gathered around us like all the dust in here. I shifted on the couch uncomfortably, realizing I hadn't brought my allergy tablets with me. When you interview a SETI scientist, you assume they will at least make themselves, and their house, presentable. Even accounting for eccentricities, it's inexcusably rude not to fix the place up a little. At least make the goddam effort.

"Anything else I should know about?" I asked, jotting a few quick scribbles in my notebook.

He drummed his fingers on the beer can. "There's this other thing I noticed a few days ago. I thought it was a hernia."

He lifted his shirt.

I leapt off the couch. "You thought *that* was a hernia?" I cried.

68

"Well, I've never had a hernia before, and I'm not one of those people who scour the Internet for gross medical pictures; I've always been kind of squeamish about things like that."

"And *that thing* doesn't make you squeamish?!"

"Well, it did at first," he said, holding his shirt up in disturbing parody of college girls at Mardi Gras, "But then, I thought hernias are no big deal. People get those all the time."

"Yes, but people don't get gigantic insectile arms growing out of their stomachs all the time." I shuddered and felt my own stomach crawl up my throat. "Or ever."

He lowered his shirt at last. The alien arm retracted back into his body and, with a careful pinch of its bristly fingers, adjusted the shirt from beneath to smooth out any wrinkles.

"I'm almost afraid to ask," I said when I had caught my breath, "but is anything *else* changing about you?"

"No, this is about the measure of it." He took a slurp of his beer and belched loud enough to rattle the nearest window. "Sure you don't want a beer?"

"I don't drink, but thank you anyway. I'd like to ask you a few more questions about that third eye."

He laughed to himself. "You're just not going to let that slide, are you?"

"Can you see out of it? Is it functional?"

"You bet. I can see in four dimensions now."

"Excuse me?"

"It shouldn't be so surprising. One eye lets you see two dimensions. Two eyes perceive three dimensions. Ever since I sprouted this third eye, I see four dimensionally! You really *need* to see in four dimensions to appreciate alien programming. I mean, let's face it, they weren't meant for humans. And I think. . . hey!" He jerked upright in his chair.

"What?" I cried.

"The new episode of *Turb* is on!" All his eyes widened in happy disbelief; the scintillating violent hues from the TV shone merrily on their triangulated surfaces. "Oh, this is great! Wanna watch an episode? Jurl and Fik are having their secret rendezvous atop the mucus ladder!"

"As I said earlier," I began, somewhat miffed by him spoiling what was surely a major plot-point, "I'd rather not watch the show out of sequence. I did that once with *Hey Arnold!* and was totally lost. Had no idea when he had gotten a pig as a pet." I dug out my digital recorder from my pocket, set it on the couch arm, and hit RECORD. "Dr. Stone, it seems that long-term exposure to alien TV is changing you into a new biological form. Changing you, perhaps, into the aliens themselves." I hesitated as a thought hatched and gained traction. "Hey, do you think we're being invaded? Not by huge motherships like Hollywood always assumed, but by radio broadcast?"

Stone shrugged absently, thoroughly engrossed in the latest episode of *Turb* now. "Hmm? Oh, maybe. Check out this plorb! Look at the gloorts on it!"

"But if it's an invasion," I continued, ignoring the brightly glowing gloorts on the plorb, "What about all the people who refuse to watch these shows? You've seen the protests, of course?"

He shook his head. "Yeah. Goddam Luddites. They don't know what they're missing."

"Well, what happens to *them* in the event of invasion?"

"Oh, they'll probably just be ***SUBJUGATED AND FORCE-FED TO THE SSSSLLOOSS.***"

I jumped. "What?"

He gave me a look of genuine surprise as he turned from the TV. "What?"

There was movement from the kitchen. An animal lumbered into the living room and sat down at Stone's feet.

I flipped through my notes. "Mr. Stone, when we spoke on the phone, you said you had a dog."

"Yeah. This is Molly. She's a good dog. Such a good dog!" He scratched her behind all her ears.

"Mmm-hmm. You don't by any chance let your dog watch these alien shows too?"

Stone was rubbing her pale belly now. He glanced at me curiously. "Of course I do. Man, dog, beer, and TV; that's a perfect afternoon. Why do you ask?"

I regarded the hulking, winged, multi-eared monstrosity quivering at his feet. "Oh, nothing. What's her name again?"

"*SSSLLOOSS!*"

"I thought you said 'Molly.'"

"That's what I meant."

I said nothing. Motes of dust continued to drift through the beams of sunlight. The alien TV show droned, clicked, buzzed, and warbled. Molly sat obediently at her master's feet, yawning with three newly formed mouths and stretching the forest of wings sprouting from her flanks.

"So I came out here to interview you," I said awkwardly, scratching nervously at my forehead and belly.

Stone muted the TV and pivoted on his chair. "Oh, right. Sorry. I've been rude, haven't I?"

"Not at all," I lied through gritted teeth. "Can I ask you how it feels to join the list of great discoverers in history? Magellan, Copernicus, Galileo. . . and now Dr. Brent Stone, the man who discovered proof of alien civilizations!"

A discordant duet of alien song issued from the TV. His third eye swiveled in its socket to regard the onscreen image of giant slugs atop a dripping mucus ladder, but to his credit he kept his human eyes trained on me.

"Oh, fame is awesome!" Stone declared. "I've already tripled my SETI salary and the year has just begun! Lots of endorsements. Speaking gigs. A book deal. You could say I'm rolling in dough."

I nodded. "You know, I was going to ask you how you could afford to make these modifications to your house I noticed."

He looked perplexed. "Modifications?" He regarded the cluttered room. "I bought a plasma TV, but the rest is pretty much unchanged. I don't want to forget my roots, you know?"

"I was referring to the *exterior* of your house," I said.

He scratched his head. "I *did* want to put in some new siding. Tired of losing so much heat every winter."

"I'm referring, more specifically, to the 2,000-foot radio tower you installed on your roof."

"Oh. That." He shrugged. "It is a *tad* gaudy."

"Where did you get the materials to build it? Because it's pretty clear you cobbled it together from disparate sources."

"Don't know. Just found some bit of junk here and there, and sort of fitted them together."

I consulted my notepad, dimly aware that the dust in here was making my skin crawl and itch terribly. I wondered, too, if a vacuum cleaner might be buried somewhere among all these boxes, crates, and tools.

I said, "So you have no recollection of, um. . . " I flipped a few notebook pages. "Visiting Los Alamos, the Hadron Supercollider, or Caltech?"

He rubbed his chin. "Doesn't ring a bell, sorry."

"It's just that. . . " I cleared my throat. "Witnesses are reporting that a few days ago, a man with a third eye and a hideous pet showed up and raided these laboratories. When did you put this radio tower up?"

"A few days ago." He froze, stricken. "Say, you don't think there's a connection, do you? I tell you, I've been right here the whole time. Just me and Molly, enjoying our programs."

"Does the radio tower help you get better reception?"

"Not necessarily. It's more of a transmitter."

"Oh? What does it transmit?"

"Well, not everyone has a TV. And as you said before, even some of those with TVs aren't fond of watching the new programs."

"And?"

"*AND THIS IS NOT ACCEPTABLE THE ENTIRE WORLD MUST WATCH AND BE ABSORBED.*"

I jumped. "What?"

"What?"

"You were talking about the transmitter," I prompted.

"Oh, well it transmits information directly into people's brains. So even if they don't own a TV or refuse to watch one, the alien shows are beamed directly into their heads."

"That seems. . . wrong, somehow," I said.

Genuine astonishment. "Why?"

"You're talking about involuntary—whoa!"

The television was nearly knocked off its stand as Molly inflated to double her size. The expansion was so abrupt that it even shoved Stone's chair back a few feet and spilled his beer over the rug.

Stone frowned with all three eyes. "Dammit, Molly! I just had this carpet cleaned!"

So you *are* capable of cleaning up, I thought.

"Sorry," Stone said, peeling off his shirt and using it to soak up the fizzing beer on the carpet. His third arm protruded and grabbed a napkin to help. "Should have warned you. Molly does that sometimes."

"She *doubles in size* sometimes?"

"Yeah. Started happening on Monday."

I consulted my mental calculator. "So she's been doubling for four days now?"

"Yep. Always when an episode of *Turb* is on. It's getting inconvenient, I have to admit. By Sunday I'll probably have to start keeping my girl in the backyard. When you buy a Chihuahua, the last thing you worry about is running out of room to keep her! Am I right?"

I regarded her multiple ears, tendrils, three mouths. "Maybe you could not have her present when an episode of *Turb* is on," I suggested carefully.

He gave me a horrified stare. "I could never do that!"

"Why not?"

"She'd think I was punishing her, and none of this is her fault. Besides, how else can she ***BECOME THE MIGHTY AND POWERFUL SSSLOOSS TO SUBJUGATE YOUR WORLD?***"

I shook my head. "Now listen, I'm just trying to be helpful. No need to be rude, Dr. Stone!"

"Sorry, but you're making me nervous with your notebook and recorder and all. Why don't you put that aside and enjoy an episode of *Turb*?" He fiddled with the volume control.

Trying to wrangle my festering temper, I said, "I already told you, I don't want to watch them out of order."

"***SIT DOWN REPORTER HUMAN THING!***"

Strike two for rudeness, I thought, keeping a mental tally. This interview was not at all the way I had expected it to go, and I don't truck with rudeness, especially from someone who lacks the decency to clean up their own goddam house. I sat on the edge of the couch, scratching my forehead more vigorously. "You don't have a Claritin or Actifed or something, do you? It's pretty dusty in here. Just sayin'."

"You *are* bleeding from your forehead," he said in surprise, two of his three eyes radiating concern for the newly ruptured wound pulsating on my face. "Would you like a Band-Aid?"

"Actually, that would be good—"

"*YOU DO NOT WANT A BAND-AID.*"

That did it—I have a short fuse for people who presume to know what I want. "Now look here!" I yelled, squaring off to the scientist.

"No, look *here!*" he said, smiling, tapping the TV screen.

I halted.

"You know," I said, sitting back down and watching the screen of polychromatic hues and exotic places—the slugs were doing so much more than building a mucus ladder to the moons—"I never looked at it that way before!"

"See?" Doctor Stone asked, still smiling, handing me a beer.

"Oh yes. I do see." I took the beer with the third arm which suddenly erupted from beneath my shirt. "*I SEE IT ALL.*"

About the Author

Brian Trent's speculative fiction appears in *ANALOG, Fantasy & Science Fiction, Orson Scott Card's Intergalactic Medicine Show, Escape Pod, Pseudopod, Daily Science Fiction, Galaxy's Edge, Nature,* and numerous year's best anthologies. The author of the historical fantasy series RAHOTEP, his novel *TEN THOUSAND THUNDERS* is slated for late 2018 publication from Flame Tree Press. Trent lives in New England. His website is www.briantrent.com.

*****~~~~*****

Got Them Wash Day Blues

by James Dorr

Panic and a head full of snot are not a match made in heaven. Not usually, anyway. But as I think back on the chaos surrounding me, soaked rags and torn cloth that once used to be clothing still drifting past into an already choked storm sewer, I say "Hooray for allergies!"

You see, I've been to the doctor since. Oh, yes, I'm also bothered by ragweed and irritants like that, stuff that makes everyone sneezy in autumn, but what inflames it—what makes my life into a hell on Earth especially in fall—is the smell of ineptly cleaned garments. I have a nose for clothes, as one might put it. Which helps me in my job.

That's because I'm a cop.

More precisely, I work in the City Police Department Laundry Division, official rank an SCI—Soiled Clothes Investigator. My job is to monitor public laundromats, to make sure the washers and dryers are running properly. That the soap and detergent machines are sufficiently stocked at all times. That, in short, clothing that goes into these places comes out pristinely clean, every time, every load.

Don't get me wrong, now. We have a clean city. I go, say, to Jones's Wash House, on the east side, I find

77

something wrong. I just go to Jones then. I say something like, "Jones, the rinse cycle on machine number eight seems a little fast. I see traces of soap scum on this man's undershorts. Look, here, under the ultraviolet light"—we all carry equipment like that, you see, hand-held as well as plug-in, to assist in our detection.

So then I go on, like, "We can't have that, Jones, now can we? Insufficiently rinsed detergent flakes in a man's crotch can lead to chafing. Then, the next thing you know—"

About that time Jones'll come around. "I understand," he'll say. "I'll get it fixed, sir. Certainly I agree—a man gets chafing using one of *my* machines, pretty soon he figures out what it's from. Maybe then he don't do his laundry quite so often."

"Maybe not often enough, that's right," I say. "We got to remember, we got the whole public to protect here, Jones. It's a big job you have, operating a coin laundry. One we depend on that it gets done right."

Sometimes I don't even have to show my badge. Like I say, mostly the city's a clean one.

But there are pockets.

Skid Row, of course, but then nobody goes there. It's like with porn, you know, you write up ordinances, not outlawing it altogether, because that would be against the Constitution, and we can't have *that*, but saying there's only special places where porn stores can sell their stuff, all in a particular part of the city where decent people don't want to go anyway, and then it's easy. Perverts and dirtbags can still get what they want, American Civil Liberties Union types and such, while all we cops do is watch the perimeters, make sure it don't get out.

It's the same way with laundry infractions, like there's always Skid Row, where bums and trolls and mutants lie in the streets, with liquor stores and "amenities" like that, the occasional Salvation Army storefront church, maybe AA missions, but otherwise people like you and me stay away. So we just write up anti-panhandling ordinances, making sure the enforcement gets tougher the farther you are from your Skid Row's center, and that keeps the bums in. They go out, they end up in City Jail. And their clothes get fumigated.

It's all a part of protecting the public.

But sometimes we have to protect it from *itself*.

That's where I come in. People like Jones, the laundry operators themselves, they're mostly an honest lot. Sure, sometimes a change machine gives out short change, little "business"-type things like that, but nothing major. No *real* infractions.

But as for their customers—

Well, I'll put it this way. My beat takes in the University district, and, as for the students, *they're* something else again.

Now don't get me wrong here. It's not that they're evil, or naturally dirty—well, maybe some of them, you know, of the Hippie persuasion, but most students are okay. Even when they're demonstrating and all that, but that's just high spirits, and it's just a few of them—most students here come to do hard work. And most of that, anyway, happens in spring, the demonstrations and marches and all, and what I'm here to tell you about was in the fall.

Head full of snot, remember now? It was allergy season?

And my special allergy.

That's why, whenever I get near the campus, I already know where I am through my sinuses. It isn't that these students try to be bad citizens, or are even naturally slovenly—except, of course, for what I said before—but some of them study so hard that sometimes they get preoccupied. They become forgetful of their civic duty— what they owe the *city*.

And add to that ignorance. . . .

79

Well, coeds aren't so bad, usually. Girl students, they know. Their mothers teach them. How to do laundry.

But boy students—hoo-wee!

I've seen it all, I'll tell you. Overloading washers and dryers, thinking they'll get more clothes done for their quarter. That's when it's my job to tell 'em they just have to do it all again. And failure to separate whites from colors, you can always tell a college student by stains on their clothes, even when they've just been cleaned!

Of course that's not *my* problem, failure to separate. The mayor, though, he's a conservative, he figures our grandparents never had problems remembering that whites go with other whites only, colors with colors, sometimes themselves separated in batches, and I've heard from a friend on the City Council that he's considering forming a special police Division of Clothing Esthetics. As part of his citywide "Family Values" program.

But I digress.

Around here the worst month of all is October. Late October. It's not just the allergies, which make things worse themselves, since not even conscientious students can always tell then, if their noses are stopped up too, that their clothes are getting ripe for a washing. Rather, the worst part is that many students, especially the new ones who've just come in that August, simply don't know *how* to do their laundry. Some of them will eventually get girlfriends who'll show them the way, but this usually doesn't happen until spring. The "birds and bees" stuff and all. And meanwhile, at first, they may just buy new clothes when the ones they came with get too stiff to wear—University sweatshirts, athletic pants, gear like that—but eventually their allowances run out, and they've already asked for too much extra from their dads. So they try to wait it out till Thanksgiving, when they can bring a suitcase or two of laundry home for their mothers to do for them.

But invariably about late October, the last week or so, it comes to a crisis point. They've simply run out—they have to wash *something!* Especially with Halloween coming around and parties happening, where, just as in spring, they want to meet girls, but they know that if what they're wearing is too rank, no matter how clever it is as a costume—and some of them *do* try, they say "I'm a Sasquatch, and Sasquatches always stink, don't you read news stories?" but their would-be conquests are usually too smart for them—they're just going to strike out. So, now they come flocking to places like Jones's, singly and in groups—the groups are worst of all, simply demonstrating that ignorance breeds and feeds more ignorance, like the fraternity that once separated their clothes all right, shorts in one washer, shirts in another, socks in a third one. . .

And me with a nose for clothes.

It was a whole dormitory, I think, that came in on a Wednesday night, the night before Halloween, bringing a three-quarter ton pickup truck full of clothes. A *whole* dormitory. But inside the laundromat there were already three men's fraternities, already sorting their clothes as best they could, in this case *Deltas* from *Sigmas* from *Kappas*, before loading them into washing machines. And you know how frat boys are with dorm students—

There was a scuffle.

It was at about this time my nose really got stuffed up. Something was going on! Activating the siren on my car, I called for backup, then went into action.

Meanwhile, apparently, at the laundromat, The Campus Tons O' Suds Cleanatorium, one pile of dirty clothes fell on another. That's the way we reconstructed it. But that was just at first.

Then other heaps fell over as well in the intensifying fracas—remember there were three quarters of a *ton* just from the dorm alone—and something had to give. Some kind of spark sparked off. As one of the physics professors at the University figured out afterward, there was just too much crud, all mixed together. Street soil and sweat soil and some guys who had pets, even though at least the dorm rules were against it, and food dirt, and, Lord knows, caked dried-beer stains enough. Some of the frat guys were football players too, of course—so maybe some dirt from diddling cheerleaders, maybe *that* was the spark.

They'd just won Homecoming.

Anyhow, what the physics prof figured, everything just being added to like that—stuff like that which is already organic—at some point it's going to reach critical mass.

So anyway, by the time I responded on the scene at the Campus Tons O' Suds there was a great roar. Like an explosion, but with growling too, like the zoo had blown up or something, except this was a laundromat.

Students, frat boys, dormies were running out, screaming, every which way or another. I stopped my car, jumped out. I drew my weapon.

I grabbed one kid running past. "What is it?" I shouted.

The kid just babbled. Babbled and shrieked and screamed. "I-it—it—it *stinks*, man. C-c-can't you smell it? And—"

This was a football player by his size, and he just started blubbering and crying. Out of his mind with fear. While me, I couldn't smell anything anyway if that's the thing that was bothering him the most. Sinuses, remember? I blew my nose once, twice—hell, I honked it until it was too sore, all the time gripping my gun in my other hand. Snot dripping like water onto the ground, but I still couldn't smell a *thing*!

While all around me, students, strong healthy young men for the most part, were passing out right there in the parking lot. Babbling just like the frat boy who'd pushed past me, and dropping like flies.

"Oh, the odor!"

"The horror!"

"The *odor!*"

I gripped my gun harder, shivering in a sudden late autumn breeze, and pulled my trench coat tighter around me. My stiff, soiled trench coat—the thought came to me then that there was another down side to my stopped-up nose, that I had neglected my *own* laundry too long. I strode toward the building when, with a sharp sound of boards splitting from steel footings, the entire laundromat roof folded upward and—

That's when I lost it!

Out of the open-roofed walls arose—*something.*

A blob. A heap. An amorphous cloth mass, its parts twisting and writhing. Near the top, mouth-like, one part moved as if to speak.

"SOILED CLOTHES!" a voice thundered. *"MUST HAVE MORE SOILED CLOTHES!!!!"*

The mass moved, and turned toward *me*.

I panicked. I do not deny it. I let off six rounds, then turned and ran to my car, diving in through the door. Dropping my gun on the seat next to me, I fired up the ignition.

I peeled rubber out of there, but, then, behind me, I saw through my squad car's rear view mirror that the monster, whatever it was—perhaps angered by the bullets I shot into it, I did not know or care—it was *pursuing* me.

I tried to drive faster, but *it* was fast too, diverging now and then to attack citizens, stripping their clothes off to add to its growing bulk, leaving them naked. But still narrowing the distance.

And then—I figure all that had saved me up to then was my total lack of a sense of smell, which had at least thus far stopped me from fainting too—then, as I say, I had a lucid moment. You know how it is, when all seems like it's lost—when you're in a complete funk, and, suddenly, you have a flash of brilliance?

Like *time* seems to slow down too, letting you work things out.

It was like that. I had an idea! *"The car wash!"* I shouted out loud.

I tried to remember where, in the city, the nearest one was. It was late in the season, so I radioed ahead, having the dispatcher get me directions to one that was still open.

I had them clear traffic—I looked behind me and saw a brown smoke-like miasmic fog shooting, as if deliberately, out of the *creature's* head. As if it were blowing its noxious stench at me, to, if not stop me, at least slow me down. If not knock me out outright like its other victims, some of whom I would have to remember to give citations to when this was over, since, if what the monster was after was dirty clothes, their now-nudity made them *post facto* guilty themselves of laundry violations.

But there was no time for that. Only to drive, hell-bent, one more block, two more blocks. Right turn, then straight again.

Hearing the roar behind me: *SOILED CLOTHING!!! MUST HAVE EVEN MORE SOILED GARMENTS!!!!!*

It must have been twenty feet high by then, and, amoeba-like, even wider than that. Stretching out in a teardrop, or so eyewitness reports had it later, so fast did it chase me.

Until, at last, I was there! Lit up before me, the car wash beckoned, attendants ready with their squeegees. "Not me!" I shouted as I swept through it, my own lights flashing.

"Get the one behind me!"

I saw one man salute. I heard the whirring, the slosh of detergent, as the mass squeezed into the tunnel behind me.

I pulled my car over and climbed out to watch, still holding onto the car door until my knees stopped shaking. Did I say I *panicked?* I still could smell nothing, despite the disgusted groans of the car wash attendants as they marched in behind with whisk brooms and vacuums.

But meanwhile, ahead of them, the bulk of the creature still struggled. Even as brushes tore strips away from it, sheets and blankets, coats and huge masses of trousers and sweat pants, even as hot water helped melt the filth from it. Suds cycle, brush cycle, rinse cycle. Suds again.

It was the hot wax that finally did it in, but not before it had torn half the car wash apart in its frenzy.

The mayor, of course, tried to keep things quiet. "It wouldn't do," he told the police chief personally, "if the citizens should find out how close we came to failing to stop it. To citywide chaos. I won't remind you that there's an election in only a few days, and if we lose it the terrorists win."

"What terrorists, sir?" the police chief is rumored to have asked, but the mayor glared at him. Instead, he called the news reporters in, working with them to create the next day's headlines:

COLLEGE PRANK GOES AWRY. PARTYING STUDENTS SAY "WE'RE SORRY."

And so, while the men's dormitory and the three frats involved ended up sharing a campus-wide prize for "Best Group Halloween Costume and Presentation," I didn't even get a commendation.

###

About the Author

James Dorr's latest book is a novel-in-stories published in June 2017 by Elder Signs Press, TOMBS: A CHRONICLE OF LATTER-DAY TIMES OF EARTH.

Born in Florida, raised in the New York City area, in college in Boston, and currently living in the Midwest, Dorr is a short story writer and poet specializing in dark fantasy and horror, with forays into mystery and science fiction. His THE TEARS OF ISIS was a 2013 Bram Stoker Award® finalist for Superior Achievement in a Fiction Collection, while other books include STRANGE MISTRESSES: TALES OF WONDER AND ROMANCE, DARKER LOVES: TALES OF MYSTERY AND REGRET, and his all-poetry VAMPS (A RETROSPECTIVE). He has also been a technical writer, an editor on a regional magazine, a full time non-fiction freelancer, and a semi-professional musician, and currently harbors a Goth cat named Triana.

An Active Member of SFWA and HWA, Dorr invites readers to visit his blog at http://jamesdorrwriter.wordpress.com.

*****〜〜〜〜〜*****

This Tyrant Crown

by Liam Hogan

Come closer, daughter mine. I want to tell you a secret. A secret the Old King told me.

A-hah, yes. I suppose *I* am the "old King." But I'm talking about the King before me, many years back.

Hmm? No, as it happens, he wasn't my father.

Philomena! I am no such thing and I'm shocked you even know the word—

What's that? Uncle Augustus? Well, yes, technically. . . Gus the Bastard? Really? They call him that? Not to his face, I assume? Ah. . . ?

Well not after that, no. You wouldn't, would you? Couldn't. Not without a tongue. Tricky. Your idea, I suppose?

But no, I wasn't related to the Old King or any of his consorts. I was plucked from obscurity, picked from distant lands to wear the Crown. Not randomly, mind; the King had a plan, you see.

He sent his sons away as he lay on what he knew to be his death bed.

Yes, I suppose just as my sons, your brothers, are also away right now, and as I too lie, in pain that only the strongest of potions can keep at bay.

Ah well, he made up a quest for them, some magical root or sword or chalice that would restore him to vigorous health. His sons could not turn down his quest, though they had no expectation or desire of success. I suppose they thought it preferable to hanging around waiting for the King to die, little knowing quite how soon that would be and what consequences their absence would have.

One day, not long after they had departed the Court, the King called *me* to his chamber. He dismissed his surgeons and the flunkies who flustered at his bed, wasps around a rotting pear.

He asked, in a voice made tremulous by age and illness, what I thought it took to be King.

Until very recently then, I had been the student companion of the youngest Prince, Edward. In the Court of the Old King, there was always such a companion. It was my job to take the punishment for inattention or insubordination or just plain stupidity on behalf of the Prince. It was thought unseemly to lay a hand on an heir to the throne.

Ooh, you like that idea, don't you, Philomena? I can see it in your glittering eyes. Though it must be a good seven years since I was last forced to put you over my knee, the memory still smarts, does it not?

As the Prince grew into a young man, past the age of such unrefined punishments, I was kept on. By then the Prince was used to my company, and his tutors thought I might encourage some degree of academic competition. Thought that the Prince might strive to best his lowly but eager companion.

When Edward finally achieved full manhood, when his lessons were no longer required, I expected to be dismissed and was somewhat bemused—but nonetheless delighted—to be asked to stay. Suddenly I had as much time as I wanted to explore the extensive library. To ask questions of the tutors that weren't covered by the Prince's narrow curriculum. To study the workings of the Court.

Bluff though the old man was, I suspected the King had a soft spot for me, this boy from afar who still marvelled at the wonders of his Royal Gardens, this boy without insolence, without malice. A boy his son might have been, in other circumstances. Though the King had other motives as well. He usually did.

I had read the books on Court etiquette, the political treatises by learn'd scholars. So I thought I knew the answers to the King's question and replied as I had been taught.

"Patience," I said. "A sense of justice. Humility. Confidence."

He waved a liver-spotted hand. I took it as a request to carry on. But I'd already exhausted the obvious candidates.

"Courage," I added after a moment. "Respect." I did not specify whether respect for the King, or the King being respectful of others, of religions, of tradition. Both, I secretly thought.

The hand remained raised, trembling with even this slight endeavour.

"Um, wisdom?" I hazarded.

The Old King grunted. "I did not ask what it took to be a *good* King. Merely what it took to be King."

I stuttered some inanity, trying to think of the most diplomatic answer—

What's that, dear child? Cunning, you say? Well, I suppose that *can* be useful and has certainly proven to be, down the ages. But it's not the answer the King was after, nor what he gave.

"This Crown," he said, gesturing at the jewelled band of gold he wore above the tattered remnants of his wispy hair. The band that left a reddened mark on his creased brow, despite the cushion of cloth that wrapped its inside.

"Yes?" I replied, nonplussed.

"This Crown," he repeated, "*That's* what makes me King."

Confused, I had nothing to say.

"You do not get my meaning," he said. "And why should you? You are not a native of these lands. The King is King because he wears the Tyrant's Crown; he does not wear the Crown because he is King."

I shrugged. It seemed a tautology and like all tautologies, rather pointless.

Ah—it means a self-evident truth, one that doesn't really need to be said. Surely your tutors covered that? Tsk. Were they, perhaps, too busy pandering to your peculiar interests while keeping word of your most recent indiscretions from my ears?

The Old King's rheumy eye held me in its baleful gaze. "If you were to step outside this room wearing this Crown and order the guards to enter and slay me, do you think they would obey?"

"Of course not!" I exclaimed, aghast. "That would be murder. . . regicide. No one would dare!"

"It would be neither of those things, because I would not be wearing the Crown. Therefore I would not be King, *you* would be. It would be a Royal command, the guards would not dare to disobey."

"But when you take it off. . . " I murmured, still horrified.

"I *never* take it off." His voice, this last time, echoed with the authority it had once held, in Court, and on the battlefield.

"But, when you sleep. . . bathe. . . ?"

"Have you ever seen me without my Crown?"

And do you know, little Philomena? I hadn't. Ever. This was hardly proof, I knew, as I was a rare visitor to the inner sanctums. And yet. . .

"It has left its mark, this Crown, over the years," the Old King said, "Both visible and. . . . But it has never left my brow."

I nodded.

"My time is short—"

"Shall I fetch the physicians?" I asked, in alarm.

He shook his head. "They can do nothing for me. I shall die with you, and you alone, as my witness. Once I am passed, *if* you feel brave enough, take up this Crown and rule after me."

"But Sire," I protested, "What about your three sons? Princes Albert, Charles, and Edward?"

He spluttered. "Do you think any of them would make *good* Kings?"

I had to admit, I did not. I remembered well the slaps and lashings of the tutors in the classroom of Prince Edward. The reinforcement of facts, of discipline, the focusing of a perennially wandering attention. All meted out on *me*, of course. The princes were meant to behave in order to save their companions from suffering. The reverse turned out to be true.

My predecessor was a callow, crippled youth, smaller in stature than I was though half-a-dozen years older. He had taken the blows for two of the older princes, and it had ruined him. I was lucky, I suppose, that Edward lacked the imagination of his siblings. Or perhaps his tutors had tired of their ineffectual sport. And though I was only rarely punished to the same degree, there were other indignities I certainly did suffer, as often through the Prince's deliberate actions as through his accidental neglect.

If I had been honest, though I was careful not to voice this opinion, I had not looked forward to the crowning of a new King, even from my relatively privileged position. Because it seemed clear that whichever of the three sons was favoured, he would be a poor second to his father.

The Old King nodded, as though he could hear my thoughts. "It's your choice. Either leave it be, or place it on your head, and govern wisely."

So I did, determined to repay the Old King's faith in me. And I have been a good King, a fair King. But it has been difficult. So difficult. The people of this nation, they obey any command I give, however impetuous, however trivial, however ill-thought. Such terrible power. . . Even when it hurts them, they obey; assured of the divinity of the Crown, convinced of the innate wisdom of its wearer.

My dear, sweet Philomena! Your silence, I hope, tells me you have grasped the import of why I asked you here today. When I pass, I want *you* to become Queen.

I know, I know; you are the youngest of my children. You ask yourself: why not my two sons, fine men that they are? Why did I drive them away, before I told you of my intent?

Because I know you. I know why you attend me so closely. I know why my illness has taken a sudden turn for the worse.

I have seen you at work. Cunning, you suggested? Yes, that is true. You have that. A willingness to play a long, deceitful game, despite your tender age. But so much more.

Let me assure you once again, of that which I doubted when I first took up the Crown. The people will do anything—*anything*—the bearer asks. If you feel threatened by your older brothers, you may have them put to death. That command will be obeyed as swiftly as any other.

I trust you do not take such extreme measures. I hope you merely decide to banish them. And have I not already done that for you? Sent them away, where they can live out the rest of their lives in relative peace?

But is *your* choice to make. As will be so many others. If you feel disrespected by the shrewd advisors I have gathered around me, dismiss them! Torture them. Kill them. Kill their families. Rule as only you see fit.

I know you are strong, and ambitious, and cruel. Yes, cruel—ah, do not protest so; under you what a *force* this Kingdom will become!

And if you ask too much of the loyal sheep that populate these lands, if you tarnish the reputation of this ancient Crown, what of it?

The people are far too loyal to even *begin* to question why it is they respect it so. There is nothing, no deed so heinous, so depraved, that will shatter their trust. Would that it were so.

I can see that you still don't believe me. Such a suspicious nature will serve you well in the years to come. But the apothecary's latest draught is wearing off, so let us bring this audience to a conclusion.

If you want a test that the Crown has the power I claim, call my advisors back in. I shall tell them to cut off your pretty little head and watch as they comply, without asking for a reason, without hesitation.

Your heart is pumping now, Philomena? Thoughts churning? Suddenly alert to the dangers, the possibilities, of the throne?

You claim I jest. But I have already issued the command! If you leave this room without the Crown on your head, then your head will not remain on your shoulders longer than it takes to draw a sword.

Why would I do that? Why indeed. Your poison is too slow, my dear, too undignified. As is the illness its effects mask. I desire a quick end. Clean. Or as clean as it can be.

So take the surgeon's knife from the table. I know you have practiced your skills on stray cats and dogs, on abandoned lambs.

On the pretty daughter of the scullery maid, the one who went missing last Michelmas.

Don't worry; none but I know of this.

Though all will know what you have done to seize the throne, all will know that the Crown is stained with blood. . .

A fitting start to your long and terrible reign, I predict.

And if you love me, dear, dear, daughter, please: make it swift.

About the Author

Liam Hogan is an Oxford Physics graduate and award-winning London-based writer. His short story "Ana," appears in *Best of British Science Fiction 2016* (NewCon Press), and his twisted fantasy collection, *Happy Ending Not Guaranteed,* is published by Arachne Press. You can find out much more at http://happyendingnotguaranteed.blogspot.co.uk/, or tweet @LiamJHogan.

*****~~~~~*****

The Great Mall

by Salinda Tyson

Finally Mom found a pedal-parking spot in the boundless lot. She inserted her chip, herded the three little ones across the vast labyrinth of the parking garage, into an elevator in the massive bank of elevators, up to Shopping Level 1. Like thousands of other parents and guardians at this time of year, she guided them into a somewhat orderly line, handed out the credit chips and the homing devices, made the plan, and kissed them goodbye.

"We meet at the top gallery," Mom said, "at 5 o'clock for something to eat. OK, kiddos?"

They all nodded. The children knew the drill. Honestly, they were all in school. They all watched ads. They knew their duty.

Neon flashers projected slogans, whispered over and over: "Buy to support the economy, to make the country strong. The more you consume, the more goods will be produced, then rendered obsolete, and need to be replaced, and the more jobs there will be for workers to make more goods. Be a good citizen. Contribute to the wheel of fortune, even if you are not yet old enough to vote," the messages cooed. "Do your duty as a consumer in training, so that you can be a better, more patriotic consumer when you are of age."

Jo had the most chips, being the oldest, so he could buy the most. His siblings trailed him, their eyes glazing over, gaining tips from his spending, and eager to do their own. That was the game: Find something, a toy, an electronic device, calculate price and chip credit remaining, buy, and proudly tote off the purchase in a good citizen bag.

Jo's first buy was a talking robotic vehicle, all the rage this season. Proudly, he grasped the handles of his very own shopping bag as the toy was placed inside.

The slick, recycled tote bags were everywhere, a badge of honor. Until all of the children were carrying their own, they felt shy, almost naked, a bit ashamed, because they were not yet joining the stream of good citizenship and participating in the ritual. Even though they were children who of course had fewer credits to spend. That did not mean they should have less patriotism. So the honeyed voices proclaimed.

Jo's eyes were bright. He dipped a hand into the glass bowl on the counter where he had made his purchase. The bowl pulsed with rainbow patterns.

"A sweet for a small consumer, a good little citizen," the clerk behind the counter said, sliding the bowl closer.

Jo picked a purple sweet, reverently undid the rainbow wrapper, popped it into his mouth. He shifted it from side to side in his mouth. "Ah," he smiled, sucking the sweet.

Fe's eyes widened. His mouth watered. Sai licked her lips, imagining her turn to buy and pop a sweet into her mouth. All knew the taste of those luscious candies, the dreamy floating wonderland feeling they produced, the absolute joy in looking, hearing, smelling, tasting, handling, touching, stroking, and fantasizing about buying items that they produced.

The Great Mall

Jo drifted off, a good little citizen consumer in the great mall, moving mesmerized from display to display, buying and buying until at last his credits were spent. Then Fe took his turn, while Jo let his last earned bonbon dissolve oh-so-slowly in his mouth. At last Fe's credits too were dutifully spent. He tucked a last sweet into his cheek and gestured to Sai. She stepped forward, worming her way swiftly and expertly through clustered tunnels of adults bent over counters and staring at displays and product demonstrations, until she approached a lavish, multi-tiered collection of dolls. Her forehead just reached the top of the glass counter. Eagerly, she raised up on tiptoes, steadying herself with a hand clutching the counter, and pointed at what she wanted. She spent all her credits on the doll. Her face glowed. She could barely contain her delight as the saleswoman scanned the purchase and the doll sighed, "What a good little consumer owns me. How lucky I am."

The children trooped up to the top level to meet their mother at the appointed hour. A citizen patrol was talking to Mom, who looked concerned. She frowned, clutching her good citizen bag, which was bulging. Pastel wrapping paper bloomed and curled from its top.

"Ma'am," the patroller was telling her, "your consumption is under quota."

People standing nearby, waiting in the food line, sucked in their breath and averted their eyes.

"Remedial consumption, ma'am. Return to Level 1 and spend everything."

"But my children—" Mother gestured at Jo and Fe and Sai.

"Mom, I'm hungry," Jo said. He frowned.

Fe and Sai grumbled that they too were hungry.

"Tummy's growling," Sai said, holding her shopping bag by her belly so her new doll could hear. She rubbed her belly and smiled. "Dolly hears."

Mom's face froze in mortification.

The shorter patroller scanned the children's bags. "All good little citizens here." She smiled at the young ones and patted their heads, the metal-clad fingers tousling their curls.

The taller patroller looked sternly at Mom and raised a hand. "We'll keep them safe until you correct your consumption pattern."

"Ma'am," the other said, "we don't want you setting a bad example *for your children*, and trying to *save* credits."

"But I thought I had spent everything," Mom pleaded. "And I knew the children would be hungry."

Both patrollers shook their heads. "Ignorance is no excuse for disobeying the law," they chorused.

Fidgeting with their new toys, the three children sat on the sidelines. They watched the flocks of good consumers eat the cafeteria food that was ladled in identical portions onto identical plates and passed on conveyor belts to waiting hands. Several other children sat alone, awaiting their equally wayward parent or parents. Good citizen consumers avoided meeting the eyes of these waifs, who took refuge in staring at their shoes when they lost interest in what they had bought.

At last Mom returned and passed the scrutiny of the patrol, and the children rushed to claim a table. They played with their toys while they ate. Mom peeked in her bag, closed her eyes, and stroked the items her credit had bought. She ate slowly, but at last the meal was done.

"Pack your bags, children," Mom said, rising to leave.

On the way to exit the mall, signs proclaimed: "All must be rendered obsolete. All must be undone so that it can be produced again and again, fueling the wheel of consumption, which feeds the economy."

Mother gathered her children, as all the other parents were doing. Everyone raised their hands to acknowledge the completed ritual of ecstatic buying and the cycle of release, the job of all good citizens.

They lined up at the recycling center and, one by one, laid their purchases onto the broad conveyor belts that carried all items to the remaking plants. Sai did not want to say goodbye to her doll, with its wise eyes and dark hair and mysterious smile. Jo did not want to say goodbye to his mini car, nor Fe to the robotic beasts he had bought.

Mom sighed and looked around for a patrol or an eavesdropper. But the swarms of frustrated children and parents made it safe, for a few moments, for her to speak.

"Hold them a moment," Mom whispered, "and take a picture of them in your mind. That way you have a memory of them, even when they are gone. That's what I do." She closed her eyes and stood in silence by the belt. Then, eyes still closed, she set her full bag on the belt.

The children each did the same. They all waved goodbye to what they had so briefly owned.

But Sai stared at her beautiful, disappearing doll. "I don't want to," she said in the smallest of voices. She darted alongside the belt and reached inside the glistening bag for the doll's hand. "Does anyone *ever* get to keep anything?" she asked. Her nose was dripping. Tears glistened on her cheeks.

Fe put an arm around her. Jo hugged her.

"I know, dear." Mom tugged Sai gently back, hugged her, and kissed the top of her head. Mom shook her head. "Maybe. . . I don't know. Some others perhaps, the very rich."

She stalked to the elevator and punched the down triangle as if she wanted to hurt it.

Mom paused in the metal box before pushing the button with the number of their level. Biting her lip, she flicked a tear away with her knuckles.

Although muted by distance, the soft, seductive voices piped throughout the great mall in the floors above went on whispering: "You have done your duty, citizens, and spent everything on purchases. Return home in good conscience. And a night of sweet dreams to all good citizens."

About the Author

Salinda Tyson was born near the Susquehanna River in Pennsylvania, She now lives in North Carolina, where she is a history museum docent. Her short story, "The Hunt," appeared in Third Flatiron's spring 2017 *Principia Ponderosa* anthology, and a new story, "Sister Snow," is forthcoming from *Abyss & Apex*.

*****~~~~*****

Skywalker

by Jennifer R. Povey

Honestly, I knew the *Skywalker* was ridiculous when I created it (I'd wanted to call it the AT-AT but the Mouse has powerful lawyers. *Skywalker*, I could just about get away with by claiming it was a pun on skyscraper.). Not that it looked like an AT-AT per se—it was bipedal and more humanoid.

But that should give you some idea of the size. It wasn't competition legal, of course. We had a maximum size for tournament mecha for a reason—pilot safety. But as a demonstration piece, it would be fun. Stomp some cars, put it up next to normal mecha.

It was easily fifty feet tall. So, when the *Skywalker* vanished I thought it was the most absurd thing.

Clearly somebody had stolen it, but how? You'd needed a military tank transporter for the torso, and another one for the head.

They couldn't have got in it and walked away, either. For one thing, somebody would have seen or heard it. For another, I was the only person who'd actually trained in it so far. It took a bit of a different sense of. . . perspective and balance than the normal mecha we used in the fights. I designed it, so I worked out how to drive it.

Obviously I was going to teach others, but I'd only just finished programming a simulator to properly match the way it felt.

I was pretty sure anyone, even an experienced mecha pilot, who just got in *Skywalker* and tried to drive it would fall flat on their face or their ass, which a well-built mecha could easily survive. The pilot might be hurt, though, especially if they didn't strap in properly. Honestly, if you hear about a mecha pilot being killed, it's almost always because they didn't strap in properly. Or something real freak. But we protect ourselves. The machines, they're supposed to get damaged.

Pilots are supposed to be safe. They keep talking about remote piloting, heck, people have tried it, but the audience likes that feeling that there's a person at risk. Same thing that gets people watching Talladega for the Big One, right? They hope for a spectacular crash, but they want to see us climb out safe. Nobody's going to admit to wanting an injury. They want to know we have everything under control. They want to believe we're immortal.

All of that was beside the point. I had to find *Skywalker* and fast. People take issue with mecha walking down the street, so I grabbed my car and started to hunt.

Sure, I could, and was, using the internet too, but nobody had seen anything.

Somebody might have hacked the surveillance cameras, but, thankfully, nobody's found a way to hack people yet.

Either *Skywalker* didn't walk off the lot, or somebody knew exactly what to bribe any witnesses with. The feeling this was a prank aimed at yours truly was definitely present, but it seemed so elaborate. We prank each other all the time, but it's usually stuff like, oh, sneaking into somebody's cockpit and leaving a plush toy there. You don't do stuff that might get somebody hurt or cost them a match.

The worst one I saw was when somebody painted Kosami's mecha as Hello Kitty the night before a match, and he deserved it. Anyone that macho deserves a dose of pink and frilly and feminine.

So, no, not a prank.

The other possibility was that the giant mecha was still somehow on the lot, but short of burying it, it wasn't like they could repaint *Skywalker* and hide it amongst the 15- and 20-foot-tall fighting mecha.

Maybe, I thought as I drew a blank on my hunting, it had been stolen by aliens. Tractor beamed onto a flying saucer.

Would have to be a pretty big flying saucer.

The first clue as to what had actually happened came when I finally tracked down Jonathan. "Tell me you saw something."

"Oh, I saw something, but it wasn't *your* mecha."

"Whose was it?"

"Kosami's."

If anyone was stupid enough to drive a mecha into town, it might well be Kosami. "And, where was he going?"

"I don't know. He came back an hour later anyway."

Kosami was the one person who might steal or hide a mecha as a prank. He was still salty about Hello Kitty, and he thought I might be one of the ones responsible.

That gave him a motive, but no opportunity.

It wasn't opportunity that was the problem. It was means.

I continued my search. Something the size of a small building did not just disappear. Especially not overnight.

I was starting to seriously consider the possibility of aliens again.

But no, the truth was that *Skywalker* could not have actually left the lot. (Before anyone brings up cloaking paint, that stuff works well with electric vehicles. Mecha make too much noise. It's been tried.) It had to be here somewhere.

Somewhere.

I just had to work out where that somewhere was.

Patric was working on his mecha when I sauntered over. "So. . . "

"So, it's still MIA, right Bill?"

"Still MIA. I'm suspecting Kosami, but I have no idea how."

"He still thinks you did Hello Kitty."

"I don't get why. Everyone knows I hate pink." Well, it was more of a hate pink on principle thing. I hated anything feminine, from the color, to skirts, to my birth name. Well, to be honest, my birth name was pretty objectively awful.

It was a matter of principle. Not that I was going to criticize other women for liking to be flowery and frilly. It just wasn't in my style.

"That's exactly why you're his lead suspect."

"Yeah, but. . . "

"Hrm. There's no place on the lot."

"But it can't have left."

"What if he took it apart?" Patric frowned. "No, somebody would have seen."

"Or heard. The hydraulics aren't quiet. But I think he must have. That or it's aliens."

Patric laughed. "Aliens. Right."

"You never know." Well, really we did, all of the evidence was that either A: We were alone in the universe or, far more likely, B: There were no technological civilizations who built up the resources and knowledge to actually make it to another star system. Which was why most sane people had given up on space. A few probes. The occasional crazy with a homemade rocket. There was

104

nothing out there but Mars and Venus, both of which were too toxic to colonize. Or that was the common wisdom, anyway.

Aliens.

Of course, it wasn't aliens. But in that moment I was quite willing to contemplate the idea, just because there was no other good explanation.

The answer was Kosami leaving in a mech. It had to be.

"How many *times* did Kosami leave last night?" I demanded, back at the gate. "Was it six times?"

"Yes." A pause. "How did you know?"

"I want to see the footage."

The security guard frowned, but reluctantly showed me. I could see Kosami was walking funny. "Check out the slight shimmer there."

"What. . . oh, there."

"Cloaking paint."

I'd dismissed it, because you couldn't cloak-paint a mecha. And when would he have had the time? Then again, I hadn't paid any attention.

But now I knew. He'd taken it apart, presumably when nobody was on site, cloaked the pieces, and carried them out. Kosami liked strong bruiser-type mecha. His mecha was strong enough—especially as *Skywalker* had to be light.

I was going to get revenge. Oh, I was so getting revenge. Once I found my mecha.

And the easiest way to do *that* was to find Kosami.

I stalked over to him in the rec room. "How did you cloak it so quickly?"

He looked up at me, all innocence.

"Oh, don't deny it. And where did you hide it?"

He kept his eyes on me. "With the Hello Kitty paint."

I grabbed the front of his shirt. "You know I didn't do that."

105

"Oh, come on. You were caught pink-handed. You're not the only one who can check security footage."

I released him. "So, it's on, isn't it?"

He grinned at me. "It's on."

"Where is *Skywalker*?"

"Back of the lot behind the warehouse. And it's shrink-wrapped, btw."

"Shrink-wrapped!"

"You really should pay attention."

I couldn't help but laugh. "Oh, it is totally on."

"You stop denying the Hello Kitty, and. . . "

"Oh, no. We are completely and totally *not* even." Though my mecha was in pieces, wrapped in cloaking fabric, behind the hangar, it was possible to cut it free and put it back together in time for the show.

See, Kosami also likes to blast music from his mecha during the fight. Heavy metal. He's going to have great fun with my alteration of his choices. I hate bluegrass too, but it's worth the sacrifice.

I'm going to see that little chump in the arena, too. It's going to rock. But not roll.

About the Author

Jennifer R. Povey is in her early forties, and lives in Northern Virginia with her husband. She writes speculative fiction, whilst occasionally indulging in horse riding and role playing games. She has sold fiction to markets including *Analog,* and written RPG supplements for several companies. Her most recent release is the apocalyptic science fiction novella trilogy, "The Silent Years." She is working on an urban fantasy serial that can be found at http:/makingfate.jenniferrpovey.com/.

*****~~~~~*****

Eaten

by Ville Meriläinen

1. Balthazar

The tailor's hands run over my body, tugging and straightening, making sure the suit sits well. It is fine as hell. I admire my body garbed in silk, and later, when the sow I do not love but with whom I share my bed has fallen asleep, I continue gazing at my form in the dim light of the bedroom mirror. The suit is in the closet now; without it, I see the sagging flesh where once was muscle, blotches where my skin used to be a perfect hue of pink.

The suit is fine as hell, and I am too. The years show, but they have treated me well. I am still a handsome pig.

My name is Josef Balthazar Hamfarrow. I am a senator of the Piggy Senate, a ruler to pigs of the world and a boar whose only peers are my comrades. I have a beautiful wife, a mistress twice so and scores of children, for some of whom I ought to be proud. I am in want for nothing in this world, save for the one thing I cannot have.

I do not know what made me this way, why I cannot feel anything towards those closest to me, nor even for myself and my achievements. I am an empty vessel made to carry one desire, with a gaping void where a soul should lie, begging to widen with ripping flesh.

I wish to be eaten.

2. Eyes on Me

I have been asked to hold a speech in front of the United Nations, to commemorate the 45th anniversary since the Piggy Rebellion and the 20th since the rogue nation within a slaughterhouse complex became a legitimate country and was accepted as part of the United Kingdom. This is a dark age for both the beasts of England and animals elsewhere, but for man and pig, it is a day of celebration. I do not see the reason, and though they will be praised, my words will ring hollow.

When we rose to power, for a time, man stopped eating animals at the pigs' behest. Earth recovered from years of abuse, from being eaten away by beasts man feasted on.

Then, *we* discovered how delicious animals are. We consumed the world with our greed and gluttony, and now it has turned to shit. The sun is a lost, soft lustre beyond a curtain of perpetual gloom. There is little green left, for our hunger is endless. Squawks and moans echo over putrid cities, the song of meatballs and chicken nuggets to satiate my brethren. We only live to feed. We have grown fatter than our forefathers ever thought possible. Men look at us with ravenous eyes and slavering mouths, but they will not touch us. Those who remember bacon are many, but eating a pig is met with death.

There are those who would forsake their lives for a taste of pork, but they are few and well hidden. The occasional killer is swiftly caught, thanks to the Oracles. I do not know how they function. There are only four pigs alive who do. Still, without fail and without injustice, the Oracles weep whenever pork is consumed and reveal the culprit. I would like to extend them to cover all crime, but the Piggy Senate and the Senate of Man are difficult to convince, for they have read *The Minority Report* and ignore my argument that it is not the same.

And so, while rapists and murderers and men with pierced noses run free, the sole kind of criminals I yearn to find remain out of my grasp, buried deep underground. Even if I knew where they were, killing a pig senator is punished with something far worse than death and they would not harm me.

This is most unfortunate.

3. Bloodbath

The very wailing of sirens has always sounded red to me.

We emerge from the safehouse to find words spray-painted onto the wall opposite the exit. They call themselves Liberation Piggyfront. The "a" is added with an arrow pointing at its place and the "f" is written the wrong way around, revealing the terrorists to be the lowest of the proletariat.

How could they do this, someone asks, and on the anniversary of our ascension? What would drive pigs to attack the senators? I know the answer; I have seen it before. They think themselves poor, but poor for a pig is still rich for a man. They are uncultured swine, easily swayed by promises of glory. Give them guns and tell them that man is our enemy, and you'll have yourself an army—but an army easily felled by a trained one.

Why, why, why, from every direction. My compatriots, those who escaped with me, gaze at the walls with a kind of muted horror. The hallways, always so clean, now swim with blood. It is curious, how the people shiver and quake despite the threat being over, but my quietude is infectious. They call me many fine things, a bedrock, stalwart, a hero. Yes, it was I who shoved others to safety when the shooting began, but I am none of those things. I was trying to get out, and they were in the way.

If only they knew my impassiveness is hardly due to a stoic disposition. But, they needn't—let them carry on thinking I am immovable. It has carried me so far.

They ask me whether I think this will lead to a war between man and pig. I laugh at that and answer no, it never has, nor will it ever. There will always be extremists on both sides.

Even my woven mask cracks when we come out to meet the army unit sent to escort us to safety. They are agitated, far more than they should be now the culprits have been caught. It catches my eye that they're all pigs, even the pilot of the helicopter, though hooves make it difficult to operate vehicles.

No one tells me what is happening, even when I demand it. I'm not used to being ignored, particularly not by snappy grunts. I swallow my indignation at the sight of the burning city. The human-populated sections are ablaze, and as we soar away, sparks dot the distant silhouette on the pig quarters, too.

What is this? What is going on? Finally, I receive an answer. Three of the four human senators were killed in the assault. The last was executed on live TV.

We are at war with humanity.

4. War Is Hell

June 11, 1985

My dearest Madeline,

I hope this letter finds you well. These past days have been hellish, and the thought of your embrace is one of few things keeping me sane. Never have I wished as much I'd have given in to my nature and ignored the consequences of divorcing Bretagne as I now do. Were I

110

given another chance, I would step out of the shadows with you, hand in hoof.

Madeline, I won't be able to return to you. I have been informed the alleged leader of Liberation Piggyfront has been killed in combat, but still the humans press on. This is no longer about revenge. Their war cries have driven many of my soldiers mad. Bacon, bacon, bacon; this is their ceaseless chant, a syllable sung when a boot falls. They will not rest until pigs are once more counted amongst beasts, not as equals.

They have cornered us, and my soldiers fight bravely, but the thought of the horrors awaiting the captured has made every pig save one bullet for himself. Rumours now circulate that captives are being butchered for their meat. Try as I might, I cannot dispel them; it is psychological warfare, I try to explain, but it is too effective. The smell of our cooking brethren reaches us when the nightwind blows from the north.

Precious Madeline, I have a confession to make. I am not the hog you thought me. I am cold, uncaring, even manipulative—but never towards you. It is only now I realise how deeply your love has touched me. Alas, had I realised it sooner, perhaps this all could have been avoided.

It is a testament to my honesty that, even as I pen down these words, I regret nothing. The cessation of gunfire brings not peace of mind, but a promise of an approaching end. I hear the hammering of their boots, feel their roars vibrating underfoot. Bacon, bacon, bacon. This bastion will fall tonight.

Pray not for me, Madeline. There is no fear in my heart. I have made the right choice.

Goodbye, sweet love.

Forever yours,
Balthazar

5. Of Man and Swine

Bretagne or recipient,

I write this from within a cage in the camp of humans, under the watchful eye of one young Lieutenant Merriweather. A fine lad, with whom I think I could've been friends in another life. Alas, in this one he has become my enemy, but I have established a rapport with him. He is an honourable man and has given me his word that this letter will find my family or, should they have perished, someone in the senate.

By the time my letter reaches you, the Oracles have surely confirmed what I am about to tell you. Perhaps you've grieved for me; I assure you it is wholly unnecessary. Even as the ink dries, the butcher sharpens his cleaver and heats the oil, watching me in the same manner as you, Bretagne, watch vanilla flan or minted mutton when they are carried in. Inhaling deep my doom and bane, I am not afraid. This is what all my efforts have led to. They will flay my skin and devour my guts, chew my muscles and carve me to the very bone. I will scream, but not for fear. I will scream for orgastic rapture. They think they've conquered me, and they have; but it is I who am the victor.

I am the mastermind behind Liberation Piggyfront.

The fools with guns were but pawns to me. I armed them, both with weapons and promises of the greatest quarry known to all—man. They had eaten us, long ago, but we had never done the same. Was it not our time to taste them, asked my mouthpieces, my recruiters. I gave them the tactics, taught them how to strike where man would hurt the most. The tension between our peoples had been strained for a while now, and I knew an assault by pig radicals would snap the twines still binding us together. We could only lose. Hooves make operating guns difficult.

Eaten

Perhaps you will never receive this letter. Perhaps you, too, have faced the grill before the good lieutenant finds you. I care nothing for it. I only want historians to know the following:

My name is Josef Balthazar Hamfarrow. I have been eaten, and I regret nothing.

About the Author

Ville Meriläinen is a university student from Joensuu, Finland, where he spends his days procrastinating with his master's thesis and his nights at metal gigs and writing stories. His short fiction has won the Writers of the Future award, and has appeared in various venues online and in print, including *Pseudopod, Zombies Need Brains,* and *Abyss & Apex*. His musical fantasy novel, *Ghost Notes*, is available on Amazon.com.

*****~~~~~*****

Into Xibalba

by Sita C. Romero

The grassy entrance and overgrown vines could not obscure the ominous entrance to Xibalba—the Underworld. Ixchel removed her soft slippers and tossed them aside. With her feet planted firmly on the earth, she closed her eyes and took a deep breath. The loamy scent of fresh turned soil did not dissuade her.

She swallowed and opened her eyes, looking down. The shape of her bony feet lay hidden beneath a puffy, unrecognizable bloat. Above her ankles, her dark, slender legs had become tubes of trapped liquid. Her skin ached where it stretched tight, expanding under the pressure. It threatened to swallow her legs. The doctor had called it edema. He told her to watch for other symptoms. What did he know about caring for women?

The truth of the matter was plain to Ixchel. The twin demon gods of sickness, Ahalpuh and Ahalgana, had marked her soul. She recognized the first symptom—swelling. A marked soul never slipped past unnoticed. The twins made sure of that. She would be a bloated, dead mess by the end of the week, her soul slipping down the goliath Ceiba tree, sliding along the fingers of the clenched roots, digging down through the nine layers of Xibalba.

No. Ixchel refused to accept that fate. She straightened her back and looked up. The gaping maw shrouded in vines called to her. Ahalpuh and Ahalgana expected her. She looked down at her swollen belly, but the demons didn't get credit for that. The big round swell of her child growing inside strengthened her resolve. She ran a gentle hand beneath her algodon blouse and rubbed her baby through her stretched skin. "Colel," she whispered. She would make this right. She would not give the twins her baby, even if her own fate was sealed.

...

Ixchel stepped gingerly as she descended the stone steps, ignoring the throbbing in her feet. According to the elders, each stair had been placed by hand. Countless Mayans had died building the connection between Earth and Xibalba more than two thousand years ago.

The heat of the humid day clung to her through the veiled entrance and down into the darkness that accompanied the suffocating weight of the first layer. The deities of the great city would hear her plea if she could pass the tests to get down there. Darkness did not scare her. A quiver rippled in her belly to refute that lie. Colel, her unborn child, played gently, poking her mother, and Ixchel sighed, hardening herself for the task.

The stone steps curved as they circled downwards, wide on one side and narrow on the other. Each step offered a jagged, misshapen landing. One slip, and she would tumble down the stone staircase and become a pile of mangled bones. A moment of sick humor amused her. The twins would be livid if the Bone demon laid claim to her. Ixchel moved carefully, feeling along the cold, jagged stone wall in the darkness. The stairs widened, the landings requiring three or four steps to cross. Then they narrowed, just to toy with her. She tested the edge of each stair with her bare foot before stepping off. Her breath quickened with her descent.

She was deep beneath the earth, facing the road to Xibalba. The final landing opened into a crossroads. Far above her, a canopy of rock held back the weight of the earth. She shuddered at the thought of it caving in. The stones gave way to a dirt floor. Soft, white sand marched off in four directions. *Sacbe,* The White Way.

Ixchel stood in the center of the crossroads, where the four paths connected. She wrinkled her nose at the dusty, fine sand she had kicked up. Xibalba could not be interpreted as anything but a great city. She knew that before ever making the journey down. But, to her, the *sacbeob* represented the paths to the great temples. The sacred White Way. It represented the advanced highways, the complex mathematics, and the genius of her ancestors. It didn't belong there in the Underworld, marking and lighting her way, as it had done for the ancients between the great cities above.

"Choose the North," called a deep male voice.

Ixchel startled at the sound. She twisted left and then right, looking for the source. Her heart pounded in her ears. She was alone in the open chamber. She squinted down the north road, looking for a guide. Empty.

"He leads you astray. That way lies the river of pus. You'll be pulled under by the quickening." This time, it was a female voice. "Choose South."

"South?" A new voice hissed. "Haven't you already gone south enough? She lies. The river of blood lies south. Come with me. I'll take you West." The voice jeered at her in a near-whisper. She could not categorize it as male or female as she had the first two.

Ixchel turned around again, searching in vain for the disembodied voice. She planted her feet, facing east, anticipating the final call.

"The West *sacbe* will lead you straight to the pit of scorpions. Come East, and I will lead you to the Council."

The North road refuted that claim. The voices spoke over one another, each calling the other roads false, each claiming to be true. They listed the ways she would die, and the horrors she would face. Ixchel closed her eyes. She turned in a circle, slowly, careful not to trip over her feet. She connected to her goddess and asked for guidance. She had been named after the goddess of midwifery and childbirth. It was no accident that she needed her goddess now. She focused on her pure intention and drowned out the voices with a long hum intoning from her throat. And then she froze. Eyes still closed, she took a step forward.

One step seemed to yank her body a thousand kilometers, pulling her from the center of the crossroads and down the chosen path before she could open her eyes and realize the path she had chosen. A flash of white spun around her and the rock walls and white roads disappeared. She landed on her knees, dizzy, in a patch of grass and fell onto her hands, vomiting burning bile from her empty stomach.

...

Twelve demons presided at the long stone table, far above on the outcropping of the stepped pyramid. Ixchel swallowed. Twelve—the entire Council. Why had they *all* come? She wasn't there for the Bone Staff, or the Stabbing Demon. The Flying Scab floated above his spot at the stone table, creating a loud fluttering beat with his wings. The Blood Demon, the most famous of them all, met her eyes with his fiery gaze. His scabby, red skin looked like a half-healed burn, not smooth like in the drawings she had seen. Her gaze settled on Ahalpuh. Her gut told her to recoil at the mess before her, but she refused to look away. Instead, she searched his face. He sat, swollen and puffy, his beady eyes sunken into his fat face. His skin was purple and uneven, bloating and stretching as if blisters had risen and threatened to pop his face open. Ahalgana sat to his right, tall and thin. His skin was light, but not white like *extranjeros*, like her foreign doctor, but sallow, like brittle discarded parchment. The whites of his eyes emitted an eerie yellow glow.

Ixchel pushed up from the cool, damp grass, rubbing a spray of her vomit onto her dress, and stood to face them. At first, she could not see the ceiling of the underground cave, just darkness far above the imposing pyramid. A light that made everything visible came from everywhere. And nowhere.

"I have come to seek the mercy of Ahalpuh and Ahalgana, who have marked my soul."

Hearty demon laughter filled her ears, the sound of crunching bones mixed with steel teeth and beating insect wings. The demon laughter roared of a fire scorching humanity mixed with the rolling boil of a river of blood.

A deep and powerful voice answered. "Mercy? What makes you think we deal in mercy?" said Ahalpuh.

Ixchel stood firm. "Unless the soul of my unborn child has also been marked, I am here to request a temporary reprieve." She forced the uncertainty out of her voice.

A high and raspy noise hissed at Ahalpuh in an amused tone. "She thinks she can be excused," Ahalgana said. It sounded like water evaporating on burning cooking coals.

"I am not asking to be excused from my fate." Her voice firmed. "I will relinquish my soul to the Ceiba tree, and it will slide down into your waiting hands. You can play with it for eternity. I will suffer my swelling and accept my fate. But this child has not been marked." She wanted to rub her belly, to protect her baby, but she dared not show weakness.

Ahalpuh nodded his bulbous head. "She was just a lucky complement." He shrugged.

"An Extra," added Ahalgana through hissing teeth.

"I will appeal to Hun Cam. And, if he won't listen, I'll appeal to the Itzamná."

Hun Cam was likely to dismiss her, and she knew it. The ruler of Xibalba wanted as many souls below the Ceiba tree as possible. He fed off the life essence. But angering the supreme god? Would they dare?

Ahalpuh let out a wet, coughing grunt.

Ahalgana hissed a curse. "She can't—"

"She can," said Ahalpuh in thick, heavy solemnity. Then he turned to Ixchel. "Go. Get out of my home. You have very little time left to live. We will wait."

...

Months later, the labor pains reared in the dead of the night. Ixchel had come to accept her own fate. Her best friend would raise the child as her own. Colel would not go hungry. Colel would have a full life. When the bloating overtook Ixchel, and her soul made the long journey down the tree, Colel would be fine.

Ixchel could still hear Ahalgana's hissing protests following her out of Xibalba. Eventually, the demons would have all the souls; Ixchel knew that was the real reason for their acquiescence. But, the longer her child lived on Earth, the greater the life essence she would bring to feed the demons of Xibalba. Their greed gave Colel her life. In the end, everyone went to the underworld. Everyone except the sacrifices to the gods, that is. Everyone except those brave souls who gave themselves up in the ritual. Everyone except the sacrifices and those who died in childbirth.

It was with that knowledge that Ixchel embraced the labor. She accepted the waves of heat and pressure. She welcomed the stretching and searing. She had begged the gods for this very moment.

The midwife arrived before dawn. She lit candles in the small room and prepared the birth cloths and clean water. The waves collided with one another, no space to breathe between. The pressure built until Ixchel thought the child would rip right through her. Her midwife's voice came to her through mud. "Breathe, Ixchel. Slow, deep breaths."

Sweat ran down her face, her mouth as dry as powdered corn. A cool cloth wiped her brow, and she opened her eyes, grateful to see her midwife's reassuring smile in the candlelight. "It won't be long."

The midwife was right. The next wave brought a convulsion from her gut, like the involuntary urge to vomit. Her body pulsed and tightened. "That's it, Ixchel. That was a great push."

Ixchel hadn't realized she was pushing. Her body had taken over. She grunted and moved the baby down, listening to the midwife's guidance. A burning sensation greeted her, and she cried out.

"Don't be afraid." The midwife coaxed her into pushing again, and the burning tore through her and from her.

And then, when she felt her body would rip in half, when she was sure that the baby would tear her open, relief. She opened her eyes as the midwife placed the slippery warm baby on her abdomen. A rush of joy, relief, and love flooded her. She cried and held her daughter for the first time. She had never felt pure love until that moment. It was the single greatest moment of her life. It faded into dizziness.

"You're bleeding a lot."

She heard the midwife's voice, but did not register what it meant. The tone of her voice rose in panic, but Ixchel only felt peace. Her baby was safe.

The dizziness faded to darkness, and Ixchel's last memory on Earth was kissing her baby's soft, wet hair.

Ixchel floated above her discarded body as it held the tiny newborn. Yatzil would be coming soon to collect the baby. She had everything she needed to take care of things. Ixchel rose far above the thatched palm fronds of her home and away from the village. She had prepared herself for the journey down the great tree. She had

121

prepared to see all nine layers, just in case. When she reached the tree, she did not attach to a root and begin the descent. Instead, she rose far above the tree. Below her, everything she knew was left behind as she rose higher and higher.

Ahalpuh and Ahalgana emerged below her, cursing and waving their fists as she rose above to join Itzamná and his goddess consort, Ixchel. If she had a face, she would smile. The twin demons had lost.

###

About the Author

Sita C. Romero is a writer living in the DC metro area. She studied philosophy at Jacksonville University and is an MFA candidate at Queens University of Charlotte. When she's not writing, she's hiking, knitting, or playing board games. You can find her at www.sitacromero.com.

*****~~~~~*****

The Emerald Mirage

by Martin M. Clark

"You're all doing such marvellous work. Keep it up!"

Director Massingbird swept out of the lab with an entourage of underlings trailing in his wake. The man may have been a charismatic whirlwind, but personally I had no time for him, no time at all. As the project team slowly stirred back into life I returned to my workstation, glowering at the screen as if displeasure alone could solve energy dispersal equations.

Judith—Doctor King—marched over, clutching a WorkPad across her prominent chest. She favoured me with the Basilisk glare usually reserved for errant interns. "He didn't even *glance* at my figures, Donald. He just ogled me, *ogled me*, like I was one of his so-called assistants. The man is an absolute disgrace—how someone like that ever became Director escapes me."

I motioned her into my "office," an open-plan space bounded on three sides by filing cabinets and various equipment. "You don't know the half of it." I kept my voice low. "I play bridge with Conway in Finance, and he's seen the budget allocations for next quarter. As it

123

stands we'll be lucky to keep the lights on, let alone conduct any meaningful research."

"But, but, *why?* Don't they realise the potential of our work here? Massingbird was the driving force in establishing our team, but now he treats us like some embarrassing distant relation."

"It's this new Reality Engine project in Area One; it's sucking up personnel and funding like a goddam sponge. We've already lost our best—" I broke off on seeing her mouth harden into a thin line. "I didn't mean it to come out that way, Judith. What I *should* have said was we've lost some important staff in *certain* fields. Everyone acknowledges you as a leader in the field of fluid-matter manipulation."

A voice came from behind us. "But not wanted on voyage, as the saying goes."

We both turned, and it was my turn to go tight-lipped. "Yes, Doctor Prinz? Can I help you?" Although he came highly recommended by Massingbird, I hadn't taken to our German physicist. In fact I'd initially suspected him of being an inside man, until his genuine disdain for the Director became apparent. Even so he exuded an air of prissy superiority that set my teeth on edge.

Prinz bowed slightly from the hips. "Forgive me, Herr Bane, Frauline King, I came to report that chronometric navigation has been recalibrated for human trials. However, I could not do other than be party to your exchange. The Reality Engine is your enemy, Professor, perhaps more so than you realise. Director Massingbird is too driven by ambition to appreciate that the Nobel Prize it offers will prove a mirage."

Judith snorted in a most unladylike fashion. "Nobel Prize? For statistical modelling? I'm at the head of the queue when it comes to disparaging the man, but he's no fool. No geopolitical sandbox will bring him the ultimate academic accolade, regardless of its sophistication."

The Emerald Mirage

I "washed" my hands—a nervous gesture of mine. "I've been hearing rumours about the Reality Engine, though, that the mathematical tag is just a front. It's certainly attracting far more interest from the military than a mere "sandbox" would warrant. *Far* more. Rolf Creutzfeldt is involved, and you don't employ a psychologist of his importance just to design a psychometric interface."

Prinz looked down his nose. "Creutzfeldt? Pah! A mere Freudian. When you intend to bargain with demons, a healthy family life is of no consequence."

I frowned, filed it away as "lost in translation," and continued. "Whatever happens, we have to tolerate Massingbird until he realises his advocacy of Area One is misplaced. Even if he *is* no more than a manic self-publicist processed of an over-inflated ego and unregulated libido."

"Nevertheless, Herr Professor, what you require is an extravaganza, an eye-catching success."

"Extravaganza?" I took in the lab with a sweep of my arm. "I'm not running a goddam three-ring circus here, Prinz. Every advance we make here has to be incremental, a considered judgement. The slightest error would be too terrible to contemplate."

"Alteration is all a matter of perspective, in my experience. *Plus ça change, plus c'est la même chose*, as the saying goes." He smoothed down the front of his waistcoat. "Now, if you will both excuse me, there are matters requiring of my attention." Prinz bowed again, turned on his heel, and walked away towards the Tesla array.

Judith watched him go, then sighed. "He's right though—no bucks, no Buck Rogers. Perhaps our approach *has* been too conservative, a tad too *incremental* for our own good. Face it, Donald, we're screwed."

I flopped down in my chair, suddenly feeling so, so tired. "Leave it with me for now, Judith. There are always options."

She shrugged and returned to her work station, while I ran fingers through my thinning hair, brooding on an unfair and unfeeling Universe. I didn't even watch the sway of her ample hips as she walked away—my usual guilty pleasure.

Because we *were* screwed.

Traditional chronometric viewing—creating windows into the past—had run its course. Great swaths of Earth were now "no go" areas for temporal voyeurism due to progressive tachyon instability. But *our* approach, Project Doppelganger, required only a microsecond glance across the years, not a sustained link. Based on the uncertainty principle, our Heisenberg projector generated an area of "fluid matter," from which we could *physically* recreate the scene under scrutiny—and all those in it.

The prospect of interrogating living duplicates from politics, commerce, and the armed forces had just about every branch of government taking an interest in our work, at least to begin with. Unfortunately, we had discovered that directing the projector required the presence of a sentient being who was also part of the localised past being reproduced. This crippling limitation had rendered Doppelganger virtually useless for espionage and historical research, not to mention posing an ethical dilemma with respect to temporal cloning.

And as interest dwindled, so had our funding.

So far, all we'd managed to manifest was a corner of the lab from four days ago; one dilapidated watercooler and a lab monkey hardly constituted an extravaganza worthy of *any* circus, let alone a three-ring one.

Then what Prinz had said struck home; *the more things change, the more they stay the same.*

I'm more intellectual workhorse than visionary, but at that moment I was physically shaken by the enormity of the idea taking shape in my fevered mind. I could see it so clearly, as if a series of intellectual stepping stones were being laid out ahead of me, but it was a route that could only be crossed in giant strides—and quickly. A few deep breaths in lieu of Seven-league boots, and I accessed the Personnel system, looking for those in critical areas who would be receptive to my plan. I made hand-written notes, so as not to trigger any keyword monitoring by the background surveillance system, although it made timeline and comparative geography that much harder. It me took several hours to trawl though the CVs, and a lot of reading between the lines, but I was confident in my ultimate selection.

A shadow fell across my desk, causing me to look up; it was Prinz. He handed me a plain manila envelope as I rose to my feet.

"My letter of resignation, Professor. Effective immediately."

I blinked. "Resignation?"

"This project has no future in its current form, as you have made plain. I feel my efforts would be more profitably employed elsewhere."

"Ah, quite. Well, Leon, you're certain there's nothing—?"

"Let us assume the niceties have been observed; it will save us both time and effort." Prinz looked around the lab, taking in my scribbled notes. He smiled; a mere twitch of the lips. "No, my work here is done. *Auf wiedersehen*, Herr Bane. May I wish you such luck as both past and present may hold."

Another phrase of his to make me frown, but I inclined my head by way of acknowledgement. "And the same to you, wherever you end up next."

He hesitated for a moment, then sounded genuinely sympathetic. "Do not buy flowers, Donald, they will go to waste." Prinz bowed, turned, and walked away before I could make sense of that, let alone reply. I watched him stride across the lab and out of our lives.

With a shake of my head I sat down and began sending out emails requesting a departmental budget conference early next morning, using the highest priority. Then I sat, worrying at a fingernail, while the confirmations trickled in. Everyone on my target list would be there.

That night I slept better than I'd done in months.

...

The Horst Energie archology lay far out in the wilds of New Mexico. Not quite off the map, but you could definitely see the edge from here. It consisted of four self-contained research and development compounds, with ours, Area Three, facing east. In terms of "splendid isolation" we could have been on Mars. I drew some scant comfort from the fact that should my plan result in catastrophic failure then the loss of life would be limited.

I called the meeting to order and stood with my back to the large picture window. Dawn was a pink glow behind Mesa Umbra. I looked around the assembly— Judith King from Fluid-Matter Manipulation, Taig from Energy Provision, McMaster from Compound Security, Hastings from Heisenberg Control, Bergman from Imprint Configuration.

"We are all failures." A raised hand silenced the murmur of surprise and annoyance. "Each and every one of us has failed to realise our full potential. It could have been a research fellowship that went to someone less deserving, perhaps a promising project that ultimately led nowhere, or even an aspect of our personal lives that derailed career development. Whatever the reason, whatever the excuse, once we stepped off that Yellow Brick Road there was no way back to the Emerald City."

Again a murmur of discontent ran around the room, and again I raised my hand. Sullen resentment was the facial expression of choice amongst my colleagues, peppered with angry curiosity.

I gave them my warmest smile. "But I can give us, all of us, a second chance."

Judith arched an eyebrow. "Meaning?"

"Meaning that I intend to turn the clock back thirty-three years, seven months, and sixteen days. To a point in my personal life when rejection caused me to change jobs, thus missing out on inclusion in the Lucifer Expedition. A point from which my career path never recovered. I don't intend on making the same mistake twice. But I will need your help."

Silence.

When Judith spoke there was genuine concern in her voice. "Donald, recreating a lost love won't help matters, really it won't. If this girl—"

"Jennifer. Jennifer Weise."

"If Jennifer rejected your younger, fitter, self, what chance will you have now, as a middle-aged man in a sedentary occupation? Tearing her from her own time would be both cruel and heartless. And what about the younger version of yourself? What will you do with *him*?"

But I wasn't really listening. I'd taken Jennifer a bouquet of carnations—*how had Prinz known*?

I snapped back to the here-and-now. "I propose we set the projection aperture to 360 degrees with a focal distance of Sol Lagrange One.

Silence.

Everyone looked to Hastings. He shuddered and wiped his mouth with a hand that trembled. "It will take just over five seconds for a destabilisation wave created at that point to reach us. It requires approximately four seconds to establish a link and transmit an imprint. Jesus, Bane, you want to recreate the entire *planet*?"

I nodded. "Both the Earth and the Moon, yes."

Bedlam.

I gave silent thanks for the conference room sound-proofing, as everyone engaged in a "full and frank exchange of ideas." I hadn't had so much abuse directed at me since my sophomore year on the college football team.

Finally Judith made herself heard. "Don, this is madness, or chronic wish-fulfilment, or both. This Emerald City of yours is no less a mirage than Massingbird's Nobel Prize. It's simply unrealistic!"

I waved everyone back to their seats. "Listen, just *listen* to me for a moment! Physical time-travel has always been considered impossible, but I've realised it's simply a question of *scale*. The more things change, the more they stay the same, right? So if *everything* changes then *nothing* is different, as there is no external observer. No anomaly, no paradox, no temporal backlash."

Taig laughed; a bitter bark devoid of any humour. "This is so far beyond megalomania that I hardly know where to begin." He took a deep breath. "OK, even allowing for orbital displacement, this new-old world of yours is going to notice some damn weird anomalies in the solar system. Unidentified deep-space satellites, comet track misalignment, not to mention Mars colony. How the hell is an Earth of thirty-odd years ago supposed to deal with *that*?"

"You're not thinking big picture, Peter. Our lab is the most heavily shielded place on Earth. Christ, even neutrinos can't get through the door without a written invitation. And why? Because Doctor King has deduced that Heisenberg destabilisation also affects Dark Matter, and that flows like water, invisible, almost undetectable, throughout the universe. Our imprint will also spread *outward*, triggering a conversion chain-reaction until it runs out of source matter in the interstellar void. Everything, *everything*, in our solar system will revert to how it was three decades ago. Oh, sure, there will be some minor anomalies in stellar cartography, but nothing that can't be explained away as observation error or equipment tolerance."

McMaster cleared his throat. "You're talking about erasing everyone born in the last thirty years, about rolling back the entire gamut of human endeavour. The enormity of this doesn't give you pause?"

"And what has the last thirty years brought us but a bitter harvest of frustration and disappointment? As I said, I've studied your backgrounds, carefully selected you as representatives from each key area required to make this plan work." I leaned forward, resting my hands on the conference table, looking at each of them in turn. "Think about it for a moment. None of us have children, or even significant others, past or present. We each concentrated on our careers and ended up being short-changed by an indifferent corporate world. What loyalty do we owe to a reality that refuses to recognise our true worth?"

Judith glared at me. "If not us then what of our friends, colleagues? Years of happy marriage, children, grandchildren, all to be swept away simply because you're a bad loser?"

"Not if you believe in destiny, Judith, or if you're a romantic. If it was meant to be then these couples will find each other, regardless of random chance, or even causality."

No one said anything, and hesitation was all I needed.

"I'll act as navigator between past and present. That means my recreated, younger, self will remember this future, and how to avoid it. Well, in theory, the imprint link won't terminate naturally, so the shared consciousness shouldn't dissipate. Exactly what kind of hybrid 'me' will result is impossible to predict, but I've memorised your personal details from that time. But whether the past versions of yourselves listen to my advice or heed my warnings is in the lap of the Gods."

They exchanged wary glances, no one wanting to be the first to speak, to align themselves openly with the monster standing before them. I saw a few shrugs, a few nods, but that was all—until Taig took a deep breath and released it slowly. "But it all comes down to energy, Professor. The site reactors won't produce one-tenth of what this plan requires. You need Prometheus."

Area Three also served as a receptor site from the Horst prototype stellar array. It harvested coronal ejections and sent the resulting energy back to Earth using a microwave resonance emitter. Sometimes there *were* advantages in being the test-bed for bleeding-edge technology, after all.

"Yes, I—*we*—need Prometheus. The technical specifications indicate it can deliver a ten-to-the-ninth transmission beam, more than adequate for a Heisenberg projection of this magnitude. Or are you saying this is all just corporate wishful thinking?"

He stroked his chin. "Both the satellite and orbital relay stations are examples of brute-force engineering, in case Prometheus encounters an unexpected solar flare and has to suck it up, so to speak. So, *yes*, the infrastructure can cope, but, *no*, it can't deliver."

My heart skipped a beat. "Oh? How so?"

"Solar matter density. It would require a sustained coronal intake far in excess of anything we've encountered to date. I'm sorry, Professor, but your plan is just a pipe-dream."

The solution was so obvious I felt like a giant in the midst of intellectual pygmies. I stood upright, feeling warmth on the back of my neck, conscious of being silhouetted against the last dawn this world would ever see. Perhaps it was megalomania, but I spread my arms wide in a Christ-like stance, and smiled.

"Then set the controls for the heart of the sun."

###

About the Author

Martin Clark is from Dumfries, in southwest Scotland. He's the author of supernatural noir novellas, originally published by Eggplant Literary Productions. Martin's first novel, *Whisper My Name,* is available on Kindle from Amazon. He's also had short stories published in other Third Flatiron anthologies and e-magazines such as *Nebula Rift* (now *Storyteller*), *Timeless Tales, Kraxon Magazine,* and *Mythaxis.*

*****~~~~~*****

TidBits

by Sharon Diane King

Once upon a not-so-antique time, there dwelt, in a wrecked condominium in the darkest part of an abandoned city, a family of unspeakably monstrous DreadFulls.

They came to inhabit these ruins soon after a preponderance of foolish mortals chose as their ruler a vapid, puffed-out, chittering being who inhabited a luxury vessel that was simultaneously sinking and flaming out. The global cataclysm that resulted from this disastrous reign unleashed an abundance of horrors from times past, horrors thrown up, undigested and reeking, from the bowels of the earth. Humanity, which had previously denied the very existence of such horrors—or indeed of abysmal things in general—was speedily conquered and subjugated. And thus began the new, near-unutterably (there being few to utter) grim rule of DreadFulls in the world.

Among the clusters of horrendousness across the globe were the Foul Four inhabiting the crumbling condo: two elder DreadFulls, and two younger ones. The elder pair disdained all but a few attachments to the creatures they had vanquished, but the younger pair had affected human names and genders, just for the savage mockery of it. The faded-sepia-toned creature covered in knobby,

135

armlike appendages was named Han(d)s; the pedunculate slobbering younger DreadFull with the verdigris-copper hue was known as Paenny. The younger pair did not, it was sadly true, get on well with their elders. Indeed the older DreadFulls quarrelled bitterly over the younger ones' insatiable appetites, more than once chiding the unhallowed underlings for dining on far too many human beings. Humans, of course, were fewer and fewer to be found. Most had perished in the conflagrations that followed the arrival of the DreadFulls or died at their own hands before their entrapment and subsequent leisurely consumption, in pieces great and small, by their monstrous captors. For food, the DreadFulls as often as not had to turn to the last remaining denizens of the forsaken city: small rodents and oversized roaches. At least the latter had a nice crunch to them.

This humble diet did not, however, satisfy the ever-hungering older DreadFulls, and they plotted a way to clear their lesser kinsfolk from the dinner queue.

The younger DreadFulls, for their part, were only too aware that their presence was unwelcome, and shambled about well on their guard lest evil befall them. (This was perforce all but guaranteed, it being a DreadFull household.)

One mist-dreary day, when the sadly ever-lessening stink of putrefaction was wafting gently around the city, the two elder DreadFulls took the younger ones out on what the former denizens of the earth had termed a picnic. They went far from their condo, through bleak alleys and derelict shopping arenas, past burnt-out diners and crumbling mini-malls, into the outskirts of the city. Han(d)s and Paenny were delightedly gape-jawed (if they could be said to have jaws) at all the destruction around them: the once-high towers now lying in jagged pieces on the ground, the small lower dwellings caved into burnt-out shells or smashed to bits. At length, they came to a clearing with concrete pilings and fallen girders. From their basket of provisions, the elder DreadFulls brought out a few morsels of decaying animal carcasses and set them inside a small rectangular blue hut nearby. The hut seemed one of the most glorious of human constructions, consisting as it did of an oval fold-down table set over a plastic-edged, delectably fetid pool. It even had a rolling dispenser of paper strips, presumably to serve as napkins. It appeared a monstrously perfect place for a DreadFull meal.

The senior DreadFulls suggested—nay, insisted—that the junior ones enter first. Han(d)s and Paenny did as they were bidden, finding the little hut quite a tight fit, if a very cozy place to dine.

But that day, there was to be no picnic.

For no sooner had the two entered than the elder DreadFulls slammed the door shut, jammed a sturdy piece of wood into the fitted opening, and fled. They hastened back to their condo, packed a small valise, and departed, presumably to grayer pastures.

Finding themselves trapped, Han(d)s and Paenny struggled mightily, throwing themselves against the door. It did not budge. They tried to rip open the tiny air-slits at the top of the little blue hut, also to no avail. They even investigated the rank-smelling pool that lay underneath the small round table, looking for a way out from underneath. None could be found. In the struggle, however, the hut, which was none too heavily built, fell over on its side. The fall dislodged the piece of wood holding the door fast, and it burst open.

The two younger DreadFulls were free. Covered in noxious sludge, but free.

It was hard to say which circumstance delighted them more.

The two gazed about them, perplexed. It was not as if they had not made some advance preparation to their abandonment: Han(d)s had, as they wended their way through the decaying metropolis, stealthily let fall small bits of rotted rat flesh, to serve as a trail back. It would have worked perfectly, had a few crows and sundry insects not whisked each scrap away, feasting as they had not for a long time. There was not one tiny piece, not one tidbit left to show them the path back to their dwelling.

In dismay, the two turned to each other for counsel. Paenny urged they set out even further into the grim unknown. There, perhaps they might find shelter—though they didn't actually need it—and food, and in any case would be far away from the elder DreadFulls that had wanted no part of them. Han(d)s agreed.

The two headed into the darkening terrain outside the city. The further they went, the more forbidding it appeared to them, with tall leafy trees, lush verdant grasses, and flowering bushes beset with birds that chirped with unnerving cheerfulness. The younger DreadFulls shuddered at the graceful panoramas and sun-dappled greenswards the humans had favored in their heyday. They were glad to see these abominations were somewhat rare, however, especially in the places humans had inhabited towards the end of their infestation.

The two journeyed on. Just as a comforting darkness had nearly blotted out the discomfiting charm of the countryside, the two came to a homely-looking cottage surrounded by oak trees. There was smoke curling out of the chimney, and soft lamplight in the window. These rustic features piqued their interest, though they also aroused in them a vague disquiet.

As they approached, a few odd details caught their many eyes.

The cottage had at first seemed made of stone. Yet as the two neared, they perceived that the exterior walls were set in irregularly strange yet familiar shapes, with a hint of florid color coming through the gloom. An unmistakably entrancing odor drifted all around them. Curious, Han(d)s poked a wall with one of his many limbs. It oozed red, ever so slightly. Squeal-slobbering a little, Paenny wrenched off one of the low eaves from the roof and examined it closely.

"It's flesh! Fresh flesh!" Paenny exclaimed with glee. "A liver, if I'm not mistaken." The gray-green Dreadfull greedily devoured it, each of the several mouths smacking as drool coursed down as many undulating chins. "Still bloody, too!"

Indeed, the idyllic dwelling was fashioned entirely of human body parts. Some were running with gore, some still had gobs of fat clinging to them, rancid and yellow and tender.

"Why, here's a femur!" Paenny's companion rejoined, and tore off a porch column. The meaty bone passed from limb to limb, Han(d)s licking each appendage to better savor the taste. "With sinews and muscles still dangling! What a treat!"

The pair continued to consume bits and pieces from the charming charnel house. They nibbled at window-panes made of parchment-thin skin, munching away until not one pane was left. They pried off a semi-bloated right hand that had been gaily set into the door as a doorknob, sharing the stiffened fingers between them, with knuckles that popped like grapes in the mouth. It was the best human flesh they had sampled in aeons. Paenny broke off a toothsome lower jaw jutting out near the front door, seemingly placed there as a flagpole-holder. Han(d)s plucked the still-bleeding heart out of a load-bearing wall and held it up admiringly before them both, before slipping it into his great maw, crunching merrily.

Then the wall crumpled. The entire front porch collapsed, dropping like a fallen face.

In the chaos that followed, they heard a shriek. Out from the back of the house ran a tall, skinny old woman clad in a long black dress. Her skin was darkly bronze, like sticks of cinnamon; her long grey-white hair flew in frizzed locks barely contained by a broad-brimmed silk hat. Her eyes were snapping black, but with a twinkle in their depths, one which Han(d)s and Paenny found most unsettling.

In one hand she held a long pole tipped with long curving spikes, like a giant treble hook. She pointed it at them, shaking it menacingly.

"Who are you? What have you done to my house?"

The two younger DreadFulls, blood still dripping from limbs and mouths, stood silent, their multiples eyes downcast. This was not, in fact, because they were filled with shame. No, they were transfixed by other eyes, eyes of brown and green and blue, set like sentinel cobblestones in the walkway, all staring back at them. Paenny started as a hazel one winked at the pair.

Han(d)s was the first to find and use the garbled sounds that passed for his voice. "Puny human, we merely saw this place and hungered!"

"It is our right to eat it up, down to the very last tidbit!" added Paenny.

"Well, we'll just see about that," retorted the old wise-woman. "This is MY house. You'll pay for this, believe you me!"

In a trice she had hooked them both with her pole and hauled them, flailing helplessly, to a room at the back of the house behind a hidden door. She threw them into iron cages and padlocked them well. Then she left the room, securing it behind her.

There the pair of DreadFulls remained, alone and ignored.

The two were astonished at their capture, and desperate to escape their prison. But as their tentacles fumbled about within their confined quarters, they discovered that the bars and roof were thoroughly reinforced with the newfangled *antidespicium*, a substance just coming on the market as the elder DreadFulls claimed their lordship over the earth. Han(d)s's numberless arms and Paenny's green-crusted skin literally shrank back, curling away as if burned, with each contact. Even worse, no sustenance was forthcoming. So though the DreadFulls had been well stuffed before their incarceration, they were soon quite famished.

They were imprisoned two long nights, and two even longer, odiously bucolic days. All the while, they heard a great commotion below them, seemingly from the hovel's basement: a near-constant humming, thrumming, and squeaking, with periodic vertiginous vibrations as from some huge machine. At the same time, they heard what seemed to be the old woman's footsteps going in and out the back door and around to the front of the house. From the hammering and pounding that followed, it seemed she was mending her ruined front porch. Yet strangely, Han(d)s and Paenny heard no groans or screams of mutilated or dying humans that such repairs would seem to require.

And at this they were monstrously disappointed.

On the third day, the old woman entered the back room, holding the hook-ended pole and hauling behind her a large, old-fashioned trunk on wheels. She hummed a merry tune as she carefully closed and locked the door behind her. Then she glanced up with that distressingly cheery twinkle, and smiled down at the pair.

"My, my, look at you two. Bet you've been bored, all cooped up here. Now, how would you both like to set off on a little trip?"

They glared at her, though the chilling effect was diminished by the pair's empty and loudly squealing intestinal pouches.

"Insignificant human, set us free!"

"How dare you treat us this way?"

"Temper, temper, dearies," the woman chuckled, beaming. Pushing back her hat, she unhasped the front-opening trunk, showing how it was neatly divided into two separate, contained compartments. "You should focus on the case before you. No, really."

"Worthless being! You will let us go at once!"

141

"Such a fuss!" The old woman clucked her tongue. "Now, you look here closely. You get to choose which space you want to go into, see?" She nodded in the direction of the trunk. "But I'd choose wisely. Who knows? You just might be in there for a while!"

At this, Han(d)s's supernumerary limbs bristled, while Paenny's shine went duller by the moment.

"We choose neither!"

"You will release us!"

"Well, well. Guess I'll have to choose for you, then," the old woman shrugged, reaching for the padlock on Han(d)s's cage.

"Wait," Paenny put in, a little desperately, as the lock twisted in the old woman's gnarled hands. "First, we simply *must* know where you obtained your supply of humans. The ones you used for your house repair!"

"The bits we tasted were so fresh and juicy," Han(d)s put in, licking the wriggling tips of his armlike appendages at the very memory of them.

"Oh, those," the woman said, and smiled self-deprecatingly. "I just 3-D printed some spare parts down cellar, to fix up the front porch. My, it did take some doing, to get that last pillar shored up. Thank pity you didn't go for the foundations. Spines are a pain in your patoot to set straight." She eyed them critically, and shook her head. "If you *had* a patoot, of course."

"Those. . . those body bits weren't from living humans?" Paenny asked, astonished and not a little appalled.

"Mercy, no. Not a one. All done in-house. Blood and musculature, too—I add the little extra touches myself. Always did dabble in art. Reeled you right in, didn't they?"

"Then this house is—"

"Quite the irresistible temptation for you DreadFulls. I've taken in—and taken out—quite a few so far. Dispatched a couple big 'uns right before you arrived,

142

packed right into their own retooled suitcase. Come to think of it, you look like them. Those tentacles! And that stench—why, I'd know it anywhere—"

Han(d)s's and Paenny's many eyes made many wild circuits as they pondered what sounded like the dread fate of the Elder DreadFulls.

"Course, there's plenty of fiends still lumbering around out there. But just you wait. Their time's coming." She tossed her grizzled head proudly. "To a monster, a monster and a half, my mum always said."

With her hook she prodded first Han(d)s, then Paenny into the compartments, also lined with *antidespicium*, and snapped them shut. The two could not move.

"Where are we going?" the pair demanded, their voices slightly muffled by the heavy lid of the trunk.

"Well, if you *have* to know." The old woman leaned over and patted the trunk cheerfully. "The baggage carrels at the airport. Every last one's still on autopilot. Wind-powered, thank mercy. Just a mile or two down the road." She giggled almost girlishly. "You know how they always said that luggage went straight to the bowels of the earth, never to return?" She placed several *antidespicium*-lined padlocks on the trunk hasp, clasping each one shut with great care. "Who knew they were right, all along?"

And she stood the trunk upon its wheels and rolled it briskly out the door.

###

About the Author

When not working as a character actor (*Zombie Strippers,* Lady Gaga's *Telephone, My Haunted House*), Sharon Diane King enjoys scholarly pursuits, from organizing an international conference on "The Comic Supernatural" (UCLA, 2017) to publishing essays on topics ranging from medieval French comedies about death, to a study of dogs in the TV series *Supernatural*. King's theatrical troupe, *Les Enfans Sans Abri,* has presented short medieval and Renaissance comedies in her original translations in the U.S. and Europe for nearly thirty years. Her fantastical fiction has appeared in *Kaleidotrope,* in three anthologies by Dragon's Roost Press, and in a forthcoming collection by Paper Dog Press, *The Internet Is Where the Robots Live Now.* This is her second published story with Third Flatiron.

*****~~~~~*****

The Catacombs of Constitutional History

by Julia August

The wichtiger lounged just inside the Library door. It shook its brindled hackles and yawned, showing off every single yellow tooth, then laid its long muzzle down on its paws and closed its yellow eyes. Only a glimmer of well-fed interest showed as I crept by.

Sunlight slanted through the high glass walls and slatted blinds of the East Wing, which was empty. Someone had snapped the striped tape that warded off the upper levels, which saved me the trouble of ducking under it; it fluttered helplessly from the rail. Up the airy stairs I went, two at a time, and slid through the glass doors, through the great expanse of sunlit study space, into the grim concrete wing and the dim, swimming depths of gloomy aisles.

Mazy shelves groaned under the relicts of old research: heaped-up femurs and grinning skulls, piles of well-used academic knucklebones collecting dust drearily under faint luminescent lighting. My bag knocked a trolley laden with ribs to be returned. It rattled. I froze, but nothing stirred.

I started breathing again. It should be safe. I squinted at the shelf numbers. There was the right range:

320.40–343.098. I squared my shoulders and began to make my way between the narrow walls. It should be clear—

A Staatlich loomed before me. I yelped. "Hey! You should all be down on Level 1 for the Court of Philological Law!"

Its head was vellum-covered bone under a tasselled mortarboard. Dire symbols flickered in its scarlet gown. *Suerbaum, Vom antiken zum frühmittelalterlichen Staatsbegriff (1977)*, I saw. "Die *res publica* existiert überall da, wo Inhaber der *civitas Romana* leben," it growled at me. "Ihr Gebiet deckt sich weder mit dem Umfang des Pomeriums, noch ist es flächengleich mit dem Imperium Romanum."

My head blurred as the spell hit. "They're judging the *Res Gestae*," I managed, backing away. "Someone brought a charge against Augustus for Gross Semantic Innovation to the Detriment of Reality. And then they're going to decide whether Esperanto should be the new academic *lingua franca*. Shouldn't you be there?"

I was trying to see if the lair behind the lich was empty. I could just make out the tattered edges of leather-clad books, great monstrous volumes picked out in gilt and piled up under the wreck and relics of the library liches' habitation. My fingers itched. "I saw them listing the condemned bits of Cicero," I added. "It'll burn for *hours*."

The lich's withered lips peeled back menacingly. "Damit verliert unbedenklich jedoch die eigentliche Definition der res publica als der res populi nichts von ihrer römischen Eigenart," it hissed, raising its arms. *Stark, Res publica (1966)* glimmered in the balding velvet folds of its sleeves. "Denn augenscheinlich ist sie aus intimer Kenntnis des römischen Staates speziell für diesen getroffen—"

It was a bad one. It must have made the transition to its current form years ago, if not decades: its teeth were crooked, and its hollow eyes glowed. I backed further and faster. "I'm armed," I said, reaching for my dictionary, even though it was only pocket-sized. Frankly, I couldn't defend myself against a library lich without teaming up with a real translator. "Get back!"

The lich began to twist its clawlike hands. I saw from the glitter in the air that the lich was preparing some vague yet incomprehensibly significant spell to hurl at me, so I resorted to the better part of valour: I ran.

...

Going to the Library while Court was in session was *my* idea. That's why coming out with nothing was so frustrating.

The Court of Philological Law is the sort of thing you're meant to attend as a bright, motivated postgrad, except of course you don't, because you've got your own research to worry about, haven't you, and none of the texts being condemned for dangerous ahistoricity are remotely relevant to your interests. Just for once, it all sounded highly relevant to mine. "They're doing the late Republic again," I said to Zara, down at The Swan and Three after that week's work-in-progress seminar. "Have you seen the charge list? It'll take forever!"

Last year, the Court had taken its finest-toothed comb to a set of tedious Greek orators. I remembered the illuminated list of offending sections curling and blistering in the incensed fire. This year, the charge sheet was full of names I knew far too well for my liking. I sucked lime and soda through my straw. "There won't be any Cicero left. They should have a whole session dedicated just to him."

Zara sat on her raw, reddened hands and looked doubtfully interested. "So you'll be going?"

"I should, I should. But I promised my supervisor a new draft of Chapter 3 by next Friday. Anyway, I know you're meant to be able to get to the Court with a valid student card, but. . . well, I have work to do."

You never know what you'll run into in the Library, I meant. Even with a student card to ward off minor evils along the way.

Across the table, the boys were talking about Dave's latest conference. He'd managed to snatch half a sheet of something original on a daring raid into the Greek inscriptions lair, he said; his paper had gone down very well. His shoulder still ached, but most of the scars on his back had faded. And now he could bound up to half a dozen grand old men and say blithely, "We met at that conference in Leeds," when he next crossed their paths, so all in all he had no complaints.

We weren't going to talk about the job market. I took another suck and wished *I* could find something original in the Library. A portfolio crammed with Gaius Gracchus's speeches, say, or Asinius Pollio's histories, or Clodius's polemic, or any of the other long-lost texts that any halfway decent Roman historian would kill to get their hands on, or indeed sell the entirety of the Homeric corpus to the Devil in exchange for, if the Devil was buying. I'd throw in the saltier bits of Ovid at a pinch. Though something like Valerius Flaccus's *Argonautica* would probably be better; no one would ever miss that.

But what can you do? It must all be up there somewhere. The question isn't "where?"—it's "how do you find it and get it out without suffering catastrophic blood loss?"

"I like it when Court's in session," Zara said earnestly. "You can return books without any trouble at all."

Out of term time, when there are no unwary undergrads to wander skittishly between the skull-strewn shelves stirring up trouble and Library monsters, and on special occasions, such as major conferences or sessions of the Court of Philological Law, it can be almost safe to enter the Library. As a postgrad, you learn fast that the vacation's when you get most of your work done. It's certainly the best time to raid the Library for books. The secondary literature's usually unguarded, and most of the liches will have gone back to sleep.

Unfortunately, they like to nest in the primary sources. The really primary sources, I mean: the long lost mysteries, the manuscripts, the authentic originals. It's a problem. Without those texts, there's not much left for even a really bright, seriously motivated postgrad to do but comb over and over the threadbare fragments that do survive in the hope of finding something a thousand other postgrads have somehow failed to find. Something that might make you and your work stand out. Something *new*.

This is a game of strictly diminishing returns.

It's why we sit on the steel benches outside the Library and peer up at the murky windows on Level 4 for hours, nerving ourselves against the day the darkness seems dimmer, or our well-worn research reveals itself to be wholly derivative, or we just feel brave enough to go up *all* the stairs. You never know what you might find up there. You never know what might find you there, either.

I had reached the bottom of my glass. I gurgled vindictively and jiggled my straw in the disintegrating ice cubes. "What are you working on right now?" I asked Zara. "Is it still your introduction?"

We talked about work until someone mentioned the new Library wing, which was supposed to have been built to give the liches a decent processional route down to the other levels. All the liches would take part in the Court of Philological Law as a matter of course. The thing about being an undead library-inhabiting scholar of indeterminate but undoubtedly immense age is that you develop a keen interest in the more ceremonial aspects of university life, especially those that give you a chance to put on your hideous, moth-eaten scarlet gown. If your gown happens to belong to a more prestigious institution than the one you currently haunt, let alone the almae matres of your esteemed undead colleagues, so much the better.

I thought about getting another lime and soda, and then about going home. It hadn't been a good day. I hadn't wanted that fellowship anyway, I told myself. Or the other one. There was still time.

I didn't have to be an academic. There were plenty of reasons not to be. I like getting a good night's sleep, for example. I like the idea of a workday that ends at 5 p.m. and a working week that ends at 5 p.m. on Friday. I dislike feeling guilty when not working, feeling worried about the future, and feeling terrified every time I go near a library. In particular, I dislike pawing through German dictionaries in a desperately ineffective attempt to ward off library monsters. The language of the undead is German, preferably the dusty nineteenth century sort deployed by Mommsen and Wilamowitz. If you can't demonstrate some proficiency, you have less than no chance.

"I suppose I'll have to go to the Library next week," I said aloud, mostly to shut my own brain up. "If all the liches are down on Level 1 dealing with Cicero, it should be relatively—"

And sat up straight. *Of course.*

The others took some convincing. Unlike during the vacation, the liches would not be asleep. Rather, they would be having a thoroughly good time processing solemnly up and down the splendid airy stairs in the new East Wing. There would be adjournments and coffee breaks and plenty of time to stand around gossiping about long-dead colleagues. They would not react well to being disturbed by mere grad students. I had to explain just how much Cicero there was, and just how much Augustus's personally penned epitaph diverged from anything resembling fact, before anyone would believe the liches might be occupied with more interesting things.

The Catacombs of Constitutional History

I might have gone to the Library alone, but the truth was I wanted moral support, not to mention morsels to distract any stray monsters that might be prowling around. The more of us who went in, the more likely it was that some of us (*viz.,* me) would come out.

…

Every word I said was true. I wouldn't lie about anything that could be found out so easily. I don't think anyone needed me to say, "Oh, and if you don't make it out? That's too bad."

I wasn't kidding about the job market.

It was Dave I really had my eye on. It's a pity, because he's not a bad guy. If I was talking to anyone else, I'd say he was a friend. Sure, he has his bad habits, but who doesn't? He also has two papers out, and what do I have? One "forthcoming in two years, if you're lucky" and one "under consideration," which translates as "desperately wishful thinking" to any search committee with 200 CVs to winnow down to ten. And Greek inscriptions aren't my bag, so in an ideal world I'd never find myself facing Dave across the blood-soaked sand, but this is not an ideal world. Too many dead men, not enough shoes.

That's why I made sure to wait under the trees outside until I'd seen Dave go in. If there was anything on the lookout in the lobby for optimistic grad students, *I* wasn't going to be the one it ate. And I wasn't.

No, I don't feel guilty. He always said wichtigers were the best practice for job interviews. He knew the risks he ran.

…

So there I was, clinging to one of the steel benches in the wintry concrete half-circle outside the Library, sulking.

I hadn't stopped running until I'd brushed through all the grasping, skeletal hands and crossed the empty study space, bursting out onto the brilliant stairs. I'd wanted to stamp my feet and cry. No glorious new material for my thesis, then: no stunning discoveries, no stupefying, someone-give-this-*wunderkind*-a-job-immediately insights. Just the same old details in a different order. Nothing that no one else could have done.

So maybe it was unrealistic of me to think *I* could be one of the chosen few. I'd known the Academy was a horror story when I entered it. Maybe that plaintive whining I was hearing really was the smallest violin in the world.

Maybe I should think harder about dumping the Academy and going into marketing. I always did reserve the right to sell out for money.

Ahead, the revolving door at the foot of the brutal '60s facade revolved. Out wandered Zara, clutching a whole book in her crossed arms, looking skinnier than ever. "You were right," she said. "That *was* easy."

You're meant to congratulate your friends when they achieve something remarkable. In that first, delightful moment, I generally find myself roused by a strong impulse to murder. I gritted my teeth, forced a smile, then realised Zara must have been rooting around in the secondary literature section: the book was far too new to have been recovered from any lich's bed. It seemed to be something to do with Horace's iambic criticism. "Well done."

She perched beside me. "Any luck?"

I can namecheck luck in three languages, two of them dead, and much good will that do me. I thought about raising my own altar to Tyche once. But there's already a temple here to Fortuna Academica (they call it the Institute of Advanced Studies), and what does a mere soon-to-submit postgrad have to offer? Nothing, that's what.

I could go back in, I thought. I could have another go. I could sneak up a different staircase.

I could use a distraction.

What do they say about bear attacks, you don't have to be the fastest runner as long as you're not the slowest? Not that I know anything about bears. I never saw one outside the zoo. But it probably applies to library monsters, right? And I'm pretty sure I can run faster than Zara.

I *don't* have to be an academic. I know that. I'm just not ready to give it up yet.

"I think I saw something you might be interested in on Level 4," I said. "Some lost bit of Tibullus. You work on Tibullus, don't you? It's pretty quiet up there. We could go up together and have a look."

About the Author

Julia August has left the library. Her short fiction has appeared in *The Journal of Unlikely Academia, Women Destroy Fantasy!, Podcastle, Lackington's Magazine, Kaleidotrope,* and elsewhere. She is @JAugust7 on Twitter and j-august on Tumblr. Find out more at juliaaugust.com

*****~~~~*****

New Shoes

by Robert Bagnall

"Tell us, Grandma," the twins cried. "Tell us."

Emily shifted in her seat, spindly fingers spinning the silver bracelet around her bony wrist.

"Well. Twice a year, summer and Easter, we would go to the outlet centre for new school shoes."

"You *went* shopping?" Vijay wondered.

"Oh, yes. We all did. Then."

The kids were laughing, at her a little, with her a little. Smiling, she let them.

"What was that like?"

Emily shrugged bird-like shoulders. "We didn't know any different. It's not like. . . that thing."

She didn't like the name given to it, the sweep of cold blue light that shone from the centre of the wallscreen and passed over Ravi's naked feet as he lay on the floor. He wiggled his toes, still young enough to giggle as if the light tickled. Maybe, to him, it did.

"So, you didn't get to design your own shoe?" Vijay asked, absent-mindedly. The omniscient had already scanned her feet. Her old shoes had been fed back into the 3D printer to be broken back into raw, and now her fingers were tripping in mid-air, shaping her new footwear in ways only visible to her.

Emily laughed. "No, of course not."

"So, was there only, like, one kind of shoe?" Ravi wondered aloud, his young mind very black and white.

"*Gopnik,*" Vijay muttered at her by-moments younger brother. This week's insult-of-the-month, Emily noted.

"No. Lots. It was a big shop."

"But you couldn't have, like, anything?"

"No, not *anything,*" the old woman smiled.

"But everything else, you could just get printed? Yeah?" Ravi offered.

"No. Lots of things we could get on what was called the Internet. We had touchscreens, but not corneascreens or the Omniscient. We still went out for food and tried on clothes in shops instead of having them printed at home. We also had to hold books with our hands and sometimes even walk to a room with a TV."

The children made O's with their mouths.

"We went places for pleasure, too. Holidays. . . "

"We've seen everywhere, Grandma. Why do we need to go there?" Vijay complained.

"Restaurants. You couldn't print a hot meal like you can now and eat with friends who aren't really there."

"You must have been out, like, all the time," Ravi wondered.

The old woman ignored her. "We went to school, too."

"We go to school," the twins chorused in protest.

"No, I mean *go* to school. On our feet. Not through corneascreens and cochlear implants. Pah."

Emily pulled herself up in her chair. Where others slumped, her ballet dancer frame had developed a tendency to fold. Under hooded lids she fixed her bulbous grandchildren with a glare.

"Yes. And we weren't. . . What are you? Ten years old? And a hundred and forty kilos?"

"Hundred and forty-three," muttered Ravi.

"I haven't been out of this room for a week," Vijay mumbled, adding one last flourish to her design with nothing more onerous than the flick of a finger.

About the Author

Robert Bagnall currently lives on the English Riviera, within sight of Dartmoor. He has completed four undistinguished marathons, but holds a world record for eating cream teas. The two may be related.

He was a recent finalist in the Writers of the Future competition, and had a story featured in NewCon Publishing's *Best of British Science Fiction 2017* anthology, just as he did in the previous year's edition. His novel, *2084,* was published in 2017 and is available on Amazon or directly from Double Dragon Publications.

He can be contacted via his blog, at meschera.blogspot.co.uk. He doesn't like dogs and is allergic to cats.

*****〜〜〜〜*****

Kismet

by Barry Charman

Old Scratch comes in at midnight, what a diabolical spectacle.

He goes over to the bar and flops down, asking for a shot of tears. Poor Griselda has to listen to him while he rants on.

Apparently he's misunderstood.

Oh, *please*. If violence was a degree, he'd have an alphabet after his name. *All* the alphabets, actually.

I've a good mind to tell him this, but, well, he's clearly busy.

It's half past when Kismet comes in. Skin as pale as the first skull, hair as black as the last, she drinks us all in. A muted groan goes around the place.

"Get ready for the sparks," I mutter to Nimrod. He winces and ducks under the table, I hear his horns scrape against the wood.

Over in a dark corner a waitress is tugging at Ishmael's sleeve. The proprietor is out for the count, face down in a halo of drool. The only person who could keep things calm is the only one who's already checked out.

Neat.

Kismet slides onto the stool next to her ex, and grins. "Lost weight?"

He gives her a look full of pollution. "Only in my soul."

She laughs. God, it sounds like serpents writhing over a million trees.

"Let me be," he scowls.

She raps a small hand on the counter. Griselda brings her a glass full of black liquid, which Kismet knocks back.

"You even taste that?" he asks.

"Would there be a point?" She shrugs as she talks.

"You're *monstrous*."

Sneering indelicately, Kismet raps for another drink.

Watching her, Old Scratch seems to sober up. "I rolled the bones again today."

She pauses. "You did?" When he nods, she asks, "How long have they got?"

They're talking about the Apes, the cattle, the herd. They'll all come knocking at the gates soon enough.

He doesn't answer her, answer enough.

Sighing, she knocks back her drink. "You gonna go to bat for them?"

"Again?" He groans. Every hundred years or so he goes and climbs the white well. They say whatsisname is always sitting at the top, waiting for him. He always appears as a small boy, so *innocent*.

Old Scratch tries to tell him we're full up, we can't take any more. It isn't fair on anyone, it's not like it's full up *there*.

Sometimes the boy listens, sometimes he doesn't. They say the pleading pleases him.

Used to be Kismet would wait at the bottom for Scratch to return. He liked that. One made you climb, guess the other made you feel it was worth it.

"I'm *tired. . .* " he moans, piteously.

Her face suddenly softens. "History is ravenous, and we cannot fill it."

His head jerks up. The horror of her words is overwhelming. He orders a double; tears, aged 2,000 years, with a black olive and a venom chaser.

"He'll put their bones beneath your pillow, each time you sleep." She says it facetiously, but he grips his glass like he can feel them already.

He knocks back another drink. "What's the point? I should just sit here and rot. Let it all try and keep going a day without me. . . "

"You know you can't do that." Her voice is honey pouring down a wall covered in drowning bees.

"No one cares. They all resent me. . . " His voice is so soft I can barely hear it. Is he. . . is he actually *depressed*?

Kismet reaches out. She hesitates for a second, then tucks a lock of his hair behind a horn.

"Where's that pet of yours?"

"The snake?" He shrugs.

"All that crawls, crawls to you."

He grunts, then turns and looks around, before pausing and pointing at me. "Over there."

Kismet looks at me—a sensation like a tongue sliding down a mirror.

I twitch. My forked tongue flickers petulantly. The old man's a drunk, I haven't crawled to him in ages. Maybe I've got *plans*.

She doesn't even blink.

A few moments go by. Beats in a sullen heart. I slide over to them, and rub my head at Scratch's foot. He looks down at me.

"Have I got to go back?"

I shake my tail, the rattle elicits a faint smile.

He puts his refilled glass down, and slides off the stool. He sways for a moment, just a moment, then walks to the door.

Kismet looks down at me. "He crawled before anything else did, think on that."

"So. . . You guys getting back together?"

She scowls. "Just like helping him find his feet."

I glance over at his hooves. He's standing in the doorway, leaning out to get some sobering ash in his lungs.

Ain't no place to be a King.

I glance up at her. "The boy send you?"

She shakes her head, an almost imperceptible gesture. "He thinks love begins and ends on his watch, but what does he know about love?"

I bob my head, a nod. "He's never had to crawl."

She smiles. "No."

"Ah, his ain't the face that runs the place, we all know that." I give her a brief rattle, then head off after the boss. He'll probably want to talk as he does his rounds. He likes that. Soothes him.

"Leave a tip?" I ask, falling in line.

He snorts. "Don't start."

We make our way through the ash, as the bar breaks out into relieved chatter behind us.

"She still likes you."

He doesn't say anything for a while. "You think?"

The little skip in his step makes me smile. He goes to his office and gets his ledger, then we make our way over to the red gate. There's quite the clamour outside, seems the damned have been lining up for some time. A couple of wraiths look pleased to see the big guy.

It's a bloody business, thankless, but *someone* has to do it.

###

About the Author

Barry Charman is a writer living in North London. He has been published in various magazines, including *Ambit, Firewords Quarterly, Mothership Zeta,* and *Popshot.* He has had poems published online and in print, most recently in *Gyroscope Review* and *The Linnet's Wings.* He has a blog at barrycharman.blogspot.co.uk/

*****~~~~*****

They Saw Me Coming

by Russell Hemmell

. . . but on that fateful day there were no God's trumpets in the sky to announce the pending apocalypse. The sun didn't turn pitch-black emitting dark solar flares, and there were no hurricanes on land or tsunamis lapping the frozen coasts of British Columbia. It was a morning like any other, in that happy country called America.

There was something out of picture, though: little me, tottering out of a Martian Earth-bound homely probe. In blissful ignorance, the tiny spaceship carried home, together with a bunch of data, a creature that should have never been given licence to exist, let alone to land: a space-bred, techno-modified insect, with superpowers coming straight out of a Marvel movie. I even got a name—Marseeba—and when humans start naming cockroaches like they were pets, or pals, we can tell they're searching for troubles.

I wasn't the first, or the last, to be sure: Russians had been experimenting with my kind for decades to test the effect of space conditions on breeding, using a species known not to be fussy under that regard. Not to be outsmarted, Americans decided to go a step further: engineering a bionic exemplar and shipping it out to space. What such brand of super-roaches could possibly do if kept on Mars a while was anybody's guess. And more importantly, would they be able to pass any bio-enhancement to the offspring? All bets were in.

The guys at Alpha Mars Station did a fine job: it's thanks to them I was able to get my light-powered exoskeleton and tiny bionic legs. They went further—they (expertly) messed with my DNA, with surprisingly good results.

And now? It's 398 days and 5 hours that Marseeba has been walking over Earth's surface, reproducing at eleven times the normal rate, and the effects have piled up—like a geometrical sum of infinitesimally small mistakes that in time produces catastrophic disasters. Wonders of mathematics, they'd say. Wonders of nature, too.

We first swarmed all over the space station and colonised their movable vehicles.

A few weeks later, we invaded the towns in the neighbourhood, infiltrating sewer systems, silos, and greenhouses. Thanks to nasty bacteria that live comfortably in our guts, we were able to stand pesticides and chemicals that should have killed us stiff. Ha.

We soldiered over, keeping going, me leading the way.

And, somehow in the process, that ineffable, subtle thing called awareness—a sentiment of conscience that doesn't need to define itself as identity but it's still able to separate the self from the otherness—finally emerged. We saw what we looked like. We watched ourselves climbing over the shiny surface of their sky-high building chasing the sunset rays, nourishing the solar panels that made us active around the clock. No rest for a marching army that's going to take over the planet. We didn't have individual names, because—I know it now—it was the naming process that doomed humans and made them soft and weak. If you don't care about who you are, you don't care if you die, which is essential to win the bloodiest war, the total one that takes no prisoners.

They Saw Me Coming

Yes, they saw us coming alright—me and my brethren—but they couldn't do anything about it, not even fry us with low-charge nuclear devices. Didn't they already know we were made to stand radiation several times stronger than what their environment—let alone their fellow citizens—could take? Each generation is more resistant than the previous one, thanks to bio-modified genes that transmit improvements in a pretty accurate way. Nice touch, guys. We didn't need it, but we appreciated the attention.

Tonight is the night, and I'm ready for show time. I look around with my enhanced vision, ready to proceed. I've done right coming here. Superpowers or not, they can still do damage, especially if they evacuate the region we've colonised and carpet bomb it to a post-meteorite Cretaceous-style environment, in a lethal ABC attack combination. Not even we can survive that, not for a few generations more.

That's why Marseeba is on the duty tonight—in the backyard of the war room, and, good for us, we still have time.

Indecisive and as slow as the dinosaurs they're soon going to follow to the graveyard of history, humans are still debating whether to launch those weapons, fearful of political reactions, unwilling to scare a few to save them all. Talking, where action is all they need.

Unseen, unnoticed even by the electronic sentries that guard this fortress-like place, I use my graphene-enhanced pincers to carve an entrance into the central mainframe. They're not ready to accept it, but there will be no attack tonight, no attack ever. There are already a million eggs placed in strategic places, ready to be sent over the country and overseas, in a glorious roaches' parade.

I stomp over the metre-long cables, and, gnawing my way to the core, begin to sever the connections that keep the whole apparatus together.

The frame's watchful AIs switch their cameras to zero in on me, and a thousand multi-layered screens reproduce my image all over, sharing it instantly with the world net. They're seeing Marseeba in all her beauty, and might and glory now, for a day that would forever remain in the annals of history if humans still existed to write them.

My fangs munching slowly and inexorably through the tiny wires, I observe in awe my silvery reflection, the details of my elytra on the metallic panels, and I'm surprised to find them glittering, elegant, in a symmetry of lines and shades I've never noticed before.

I'll probably give a name to my next offspring. They deserve it. After all, they'll inherit the world.

About the Author

Russell Hemmell is a statistician and social scientist from the U.K., passionate about astrophysics and speculative fiction. He has recent work in *Not One of Us, PerihelionSF, SQ Mag,* and others. He was a finalist in The Canopus 100 Year Starship Awards 2016-2017.

*****\~\~\~\~******

Bigger and Better Things

by Joseph Sidari

He crawled from his safe dark corner under the desk, scuttled onto a leather armchair, and realized he was now a man. Had he just been hunting for fallen crumbs on the carpet—or was that part a dream? Now an entire donut lounged before him on a nest of papers. A flattened disc of beef and fat lay beside it on waxed paper. Elongated food-sticks smelling of salt and oil were piled next to that. Their savory, greasy smell competed with the sugary-sweet scent of the pastry.

Unsure where to begin, he reached out with his new, odd appendages and pinched off a piece of the donut. He brought it to his maw, snapping open his soft pink lips. It was good, but such a small bite. Why eat a little when he was now so big. . .

He grasped at the stale, broken edge and fumbled it to the floor. With a clumsy newness, he reached down to retrieve his feast. He rammed the rest of the dry confection into his oral cavity. His mandible scissored up and down, working it into a paste.

Ahh. Crunchy yet chewy. Sugary and— "Ahem." He tried to swallow—or to breathe. He could do neither. "Ahem, ahem."

He thrashed from side to side. Coughing and gagging, he spied a Styrofoam cup and leaned forward to grab it, desperate to lubricate his gullet. He upended the cold coffee into his mouth. A bitter, rancid slurry now solidified in his gorge.

He kicked. He pounded the desktop. He stood, frantic for air.

"Mr. Gregory?" A female opened his door and poked her head in. "Did you want—?"

He flailed at his soft, pink neck. His lips tingled. His head spun.

"Oh, no!" The female darted across the room to him. She wrapped her hands around his girth and squeezed him from behind, as if to crush him.

With a whoosh, he expectorated the food plug onto his desk. He gulped in cool air.

"If I hadn't come to say your 2:30 was early. . . " She shuddered. "Are you okay?"

He nodded.

"Should I call Dr. Frank?"

"Huh?"

"Your primary care? Maybe he could get you in for a check-up?" She arched an eyebrow in concern. "It's been awhile since—"

"No. I feel fine." He cleared his throat of the heavy phlegm that was still coating his vocal cords.

"And your fundraising dinner tonight," she continued. "They called to see which entrée you wanted: fried chicken or the T-bone steak?"

"Both," he croaked. He glanced over at the paste of chewed-up donut that was congealing on his desk. His stomach rumbled.

"Um, okay." She eyed him warily. "Can I get you anything else? Before I send in your 2:30?"

"More snacks," he rasped, and then shooed her away. He reached down and ran a finger through the glop that obscured his brass nameplate:

Bigger and Better Things
Sam Gregory
Director, Human Resources

He jammed the finger into his mouth, savoring the goo. He swallowed, and then burped. He rubbed at his chest, where a dull pain was blossoming. That female had squeezed him hard.

He surveyed his food scattered about the desktop: his meaty stack, his oiled sticks, his caffeinated drink. He had never eaten this well before. He was always hunting for food. Worrying about predators. Eating whatever he could find. But these humans; *they* really knew how to feast.

He reached down and grabbed a handful of the salty fried sticks, and then thought better, dropping a few back to the desk. He didn't want this newly found treasure trove of food to try to kill him again. He would eat it all, for sure. He'd just take smaller bites.

###

About the Author

Joseph Sidari (www.josephsidari.com) writes from outside of Boston. He has been published in *Daily Science Fiction, Every Day Fiction*, and *Brilliant Flash Fiction,* among others. He is currently waiting for his agented novel, *LITTLE GREEN MEN*, to find a publisher. He would never step on a cockroach, because you never now who that bug might grow up to be some day.

*****~~~~~*****

Credits and Acknowledgments

Cover image and design – Keely Rew
Podcast production – Andrew Cairns
Readers – Keely Rew, Andrew Cairns, Tom Parker, Leonard Sitongia
Editor and Publisher – Juliana Rew

*****∼∼∼∼∼*****

Discover other titles by Third Flatiron:

THIRD FLATIRON
www.thirdflatiron.com

www.ingramcontent.com/pod-product-compliance
Lightning Source LLC
Chambersburg PA
CBHW071248130626
46556CB00003B/1215